The Headmaster's Wife

By Richard Hawley

Papers from the Headmaster, Eriksson. 1996.

Boys Will Be Men: Masculinity in Troubled Times. Eriksson, 1994.

Hail University! A Century of University School Life.
University School Press, 1990.

Mr. Chips Redux? Miss Dove Redivivus: In Praise of the Teaching Life.
University School Press, 1988.

The Big Issues in the Passage to Adulthood. Walker and Co., 1987.

Seeing Things: A Chronicle of Surprises. Walker and Co., 1987.

Drugs and Society: Responding to an Epidemic.
Walker and Co., 1987.

St. Julian. Bits Press, 1987.

A School Answers Back. American Council on Drug Education, 1984.

The Headmaster's Papers. Eriksson, 1983. Bantam, 1984.
Revised Edition, Eriksson, 1992.

The Purposes of Pleasure: A Reflection on Youth and Drugs.
Independent School Press, 1983.

With Love to My Survivors. Cleveland State
University Poetry Center, 1982.

The Headmaster's Wife

A Novel
by
Richard
Hawley

Paul S. Eriksson, *Publisher*
Forest Dale, Vermont

5 4 3 2 1

Library of Congress Cataloging-in-Publication Data
Hawley, Richard A.
The headmaster's wife: a novel/Richard Hawley.
    p. cm.
Sequel to: The headmaster's papers.
ISBN 0-8397-3193-0 (cloth)
    1. Married women--Fiction. I. Title.
PS3558.A8236 H44 2000
813'.54--dc21   00-035447

Design by Eugenie S. Delaney

To Paul and Peggy
for their faith and work.

Margaret, are you grieving
Over Goldengrove unleaving?
Leaves, like the things of man, you
With your fresh thoughts care for, can you?
Ah! As the heart grows older
It will come to such sights colder
By and by, nor spare a sigh
Though words of wanwood leafmeal lie;
And yet you *will* weep and know why.
Now, no matter, child, the name:
Sorrow's springs are the same.
Nor mouth had, no more mind, expressed
What heart heard of, ghost guessed:
It is the blight man was born for,
It is Margaret you mourn for.

—GERARD MANLEY HOPKINS

The
Headmaster's
Wife

August 28

I don't know.

And that's the truth, book-y. Here you are, your gorgeous marbly covers spread wide like some ripe and ready girl, all your creamy white pages spilling out to me waiting for—what? For me to scratch and ink you into fullness, to finish you, to make you heavy with old Meg Greeve. Like all your book-y sisters, quiet but maybe not dead on their dedicated shelves. In the end, you will be me. All the me there was.

Gloomy greeting to a sweet-smelling new Little Book. What are you—109? I've just checked. You are. Hello! Welcome, 109. Forgive my scribbling you up. Know that I love you.

Inventory. Mid-August, still at Little House, East Sandwich. John's packed up and left the Cape to stoke up Wells into a school year. So sad for me, but all right. Blessed lovey, he wanted me to have this sun-blanched quiet time. He knows I know the train's pulling away, chugging and puffing toward June and prize days and commencement on the commons. No stops on that train for the craggy old engineer.

He did and didn't want to leave me here. He knew I'd love the time and the sweet quiet, but he was rattled by Dr. Karipides' report. "Tests" to be done. *Tests!* How artlessly forbidding can medicine get? "Blood work." *Work?* What a way to talk about blood. I am pretty sure John is terrified. Poor hurt baby has seen too much to believe people always get past their bugs and fevers and lumps and sweats. Dangerous quality in a headmaster. Better to be an idiot optimist, hale-fellowing through everything, all smiles and granite handshakes, dumb as a post, strong as an ox.

Old Meg's not strong as an ox today. She's maybe strong as a gerbil. Funny, annoying way to wake up to the world: a weight, like grainy liquid, behind my eyes, strange sour mouth, dodgy cramped lowers. Stomach shut tight, no appetite. I get up, shuffle around, bathe and brush, and—no forward motion. The sun makes ripply white and yellow fire in the cove, and I can just hear the seaside flaps and bangs beyond the screens, but all that light is too oppressive and strong for me today (again!), and I move leadenly in the direction of a chair. No fever this a.m., 100° when I went to bed. Just *proceed*, leaden-ness, proceed, proceed. Make your point, get on with it. Nothing hurts. Everything works. So why don't the wheels go when I clunk her into gear? "I'm concerned," says the handsome and unleaden Dr. Karipides under his fascinating skull-wide black brow. And tests to boot. Indignities in every orifice, in the tender crook of my arm, hot punctures and those horrible little plastic boxes of blood, clipped together like children's toys, each darkly and horribly full of me, for the tests. How much more healing if the angular and unibrowed Dr. Karipides had placed his great brown hands on my shoulders and said: Mrs. Greeve, I find you the most fascinating woman I have ever examined. Forgive me for falling in love with you. But no. Blood work.

Back again. Some tea and tuna fish toast are now sitting meaninglessly within. What a curious thing to have no appetite. An affront to living. Appetite drives the whole green world, and here is the solitary and ever bonier and beakier Meg G. sitting *indoors*, a peculiar figure, should anyone peer into our deck screens. But apparently appetite is unnecessary to percolate my tiny neurons into thoughts, words, memories. Scratch, scratch, scratch.

Bad moment at the mirror. No light on, so the murk spared me the usual outrage at alien puffs and creases and pallor. But the hair! John's beloved "girlish bob" gone straight as string. What's happened to the reliable seaside air. Why is my hair hanging close to my temples like straw? Not like straw, like dead hair. Come on, hair, be a good feature again. The woman in the mirror looked like one of those TV puppet creations—bloopers? puppettes? No, Muppets. A bird with a comical beak wearing a wig of dead straight hair, bangs down to the glasses. Maybe it's the glasses. Surely when I remember to take them off I will be alluring again, and Dr. Karipides' "concern" will dissolve into the first glimmer of desire.

Two weeks past 55, no need to be an old bird. Contemporaries of mine are still movie stars (in careful lighting), make exercise videos in spandex.

Two weeks past 55, a bespectacled Muppet with bad lady's hair, not blood but something more like dirty dishwater slopping through my system, I am still in my true heart a girl. A girl, Dr. K., not a concern.

The trick is to locate the girl. And today I find her in Maine, on the point of sun-baked boulders at the tip of Blue Hill. The little dirt path behind the boathouse through the pines is almost grown over with blueberries and poison ivy, and only Siri and I with a giddy knowing disguised as foolishness dare this path, and we emerge into a thrilling wash of loud white sunlight on the rock heaps. The water is stingingly, numbingly icy and so clear the pebbly sea bottom is all honey and emerald. There is every way to hide from view among these radiant rocks. From? From Stinky and Freddy, the leathery old lobstermen who set their pots along the shallows? From the low sleek hulls of yachts small as toys on the horizon?

From the planing gulls? No, I welcomed the gulls, the gulls and the pressing sun on my cheeks and belly and thighs. We browned and browned ourselves, in a week the color of honey, in two, chocolate. And some secret blood-loving quality of that northeast sunshine always brought up reds and peach through the leathery brown. There is no complexion more affirmingly healthy. Skin glowing in that way would disengage the reflex, even in my mother, to say don't overdo it, dear. The point was to overdo it, to offer my body like prayer to the radiance. To say yes and yes and yes in chorus with the gulls. When we baked so long our beaded bellies were hot to the palm, we would inch, daring ourselves, off the rocks into the water so cold that for an instant it blocked all sensation, then, whether at ankle or thigh or hip, it left a delicious ache that made us squeal in amazement at the impossibility of such cold. Back on the hot stone, my skin would tingle electrically for shivering minutes as breezes skidded over goosebumps and the water pooled cold and clean on the umber of my belly.

Oh, girl! And your sweet, flat, perfect, untried belly. Yes and now it's clear (again) why I return to my girl bathing on the rocks. No accident, I suppose, that the stalled and unstirrable old Muppet lady locates the girl in her first ecstatic stirring. Oh, the good sweet rush of it, neither itch nor burn, but like them, beginning in the depths of my belly, or in a breeze across my midriff, anywhere really, then connecting to all my parts, lips, breasts, palms, the tips of my toes, wherever sun met skin. I stretch, I arch, I cast my girl's hips to meet the unseen sun. Then all of it is drawn together deep within me, and I can feel the glowing mass of it in my sex. There were no words for it. How I wanted to move with it, to touch it, stroke it, hold it.

Siri, bless her heart, felt everything. In memory—could it have been true?—we were one flesh. I was certain her skin felt what my skin felt. She was bigger, blonder. The more of her was extra me. We came to the rocks knowing the same thing, for the same unstated, ecstatic communion. This was, if there were words, why we were deliciously hiding. It was too bright, too sacred for the family dock or for boats. My eyes were sealed shut against the sun when Siri said, Meg, have you ever stripped? *Stripped*. Bless you, bless you, Siri, for that wrong right word. The dangerous, vulgar word was supposed to be about alluring others to forbidden feeling. Stripper. Striptease. Strip poker. We knew—I knew it was about releasing a personal secret. Strip. It was about returning to something overwhelmingly sweet and rich, a green bright world where I had been naked forever. We laughed. Looked at each other wide-eyed, laughed and laughed. I propped myself up on my elbows and scanned the rim of the sea and the far shore. Only white tips of sail on the horizon. When I turned back to Siri, she had unhooked her top and it fell to her lap.

Her smile was a surrender. The soft little buds of her breasts were milky white in the sunlight. She threw her head back and hummed up into the sun. Bless her heart. What a simple perfect pleasure: to strip. I pulled my own top over my head and lay back in wonder. Now the clothed world, the racket of our cottage, the crunch of doors closing, the clink and tinkling of the boats' rigging down the dock were banished from memory. This is it, this is me, this is all I want. I glanced back at Siri and saw, as I knew I would, that she had peeled out of her suit bottom. Her thighs from my angle of view now seemed strangely full, and the sun made delicate threads of fire among the pale hairs over her sex. Again I thank you, Siri. I peeled my suit bottom down over my feet, lay back, and made angel arcs with my arms and legs. Then I lay still and let the bright day in.

I suppose it was sex. But sex seems to me always to be involved with the other. Siri and I, summer friends, were only extended selves. We tickled and touched, held each other's faces in our hands, played looking into each other's eyes to see who would break into laughter first. It was important in our charged and thrilling nakedness to look only into her eyes. Everything beyond the fixed shaft of our dumb mutual staring was pulsing with sun and promise. The whole crisp sea-washed world had stripped. Once, not that day but that summer, the pulsing was too much for me, and I edged off my roasting rock into the stunning freeze of the water, crouched so my belly and bottom were submerged. Stealthily, I touched myself and worked to bring the tickle to flower. The water was so cold it felt like toothache along my boney shins. The impulse to sex under ice water—the story of my life? God forbid. Sneaked a look back at Siri who, troubled by no such modesty, lay splayed open to her thrumming fingers. Her eyes were squeezed shut in a terrific grimace, and as she raised her round bottom from the rock, I erupted with pleasure, sharp as a knife in the scalding cold, where pleasure meets pain. Neither of us felt we had to explain. The perfect summer friend.

This, Little Book, is how I began to feel all right about the ultimate, or if not all right, too much in its thrall to be bothered by recriminations. Always have been. Still am—or would be, if this curse of leadenness would lift. What's it been now, weeks? No, months really, since May. Oh dear, Meg. No wonder you fly back to Maine.

May I fly back again. Maine is the beginning of goodness, the beginning of deep knowing. I wanted a Maine for Brian. *Brian!* Where are you? Come home, come home, come home. Little House, the boat, the Cape, the iron boundary around these summer weeks— this was supposed to be Brian's Maine. Maddening cipher, beloved boy, I hope you had secret Maines that would take your mother's breath away. Or is that what you're up to, looking for your own sort of Maine. I suppose, I suppose that's what we all do. Why Portugal? Why a Maine beyond my dim imagining? Why is this love of mine, this wide open, oceanic, ask *nothing* love of mine so resistible to you, boy? How can love repel? Am I kidding myself? Is it just need. I know neediness repels. But I would promise not to need, only to love, only to know. Surely it's a mother's right to behold the son from time to time. *Ecce puer.* Brian, you are so cunning, so subtle. You know what breaks your mother's heart. And your father's. Is that what you need? To break his heart and win? Are you perhaps breaking mine inadvertently, in addition? Why break hearts? Why flee? Why win?

See how I go. From Maine to misery—or is it from misery to Maine to misery, which is essentially from misery to misery. Is that the story of my life, or perhaps a preview? Should be kind to Little Book and put away my pen. Supper time—hah!—in Little House, and what has Mrs. Greeve achieved on this lovely, blowy August day? She saw patches of cerulean blue beyond the screens and cumulus clouds billow into majestic and no doubt portentous shapes. She saw the pines shiver and the maples sway. She eyed grossbeaks at the feeder, and they eyed the gross beak inside. She grew objective. She remembered the erotic but could not feel it. She grieved for her little Greeve, her little grief. God, stop it. Scratch, scratch, scratch. Now on to non-supper. Still no temperature.

August 29

Grey and soupy day, both outside and in. I was 99.5° this a.m., if I read the new thermometer right. Not a very impressive temperature, but sufficient to describe this head-full-of-soot feeling. Amazing. I find myself longing to erupt into some spectacular symptoms. Perfect phrase: under the weather. I am under the weather as a potato bug is under a damp log. I am shunning the mirror for the time being, because I don't want to look at a potato bug. Thought I might renew my resolve to flush out the lead with preposterous doses of water and fruit juice. So far this has resulted only in leadenness with constant peeing. Being "proactive"—horrible neologism—doesn't show me much. Bugger off, malaise.

Call last night from John left me sad. No word from Brian. I could hear John not wanting to tell me this. Departed children. No ache, no clasping void like this. Why are we made to hurt like this when, in some more or less socially acceptable way, children leave us. Why do we have them? To have them and lose them. God, teach me why having implies losing. Must everything negate? Why negate one's own body food, a baby, a boy, my Brian, my Brian. John's not wanting me to feel this succeeds only in dissolving me. I know he is sick with it, numb with it. He tries to absent himself, to isolate the Brian hurt as one kind of hurt among the world's knowable hurts. Poor dear wants to figure it out. He doesn't know, doesn't want to know that this loss is pre-word, pre-name. Only a man would cry out Absalom, Absalom. A woman just cries, cries in. Having implies losing. Know this, you apple-cheeked, sun-bleached beauties toting your sausage-limbed treasures through the East Sandwich general store. They detach, they go away.

John talks of opening up and de-musting the house, the bright cycles of pre-season workouts and cook-outs and orientations. I can somehow hear the clamor, the thud of cleats on the hard summer turf. Who is it, the coaches, who turned the impulse to play into such ferocious work? Who knows, to them it may be play. Even picturing it makes me so tired. Poor John, I think it makes him tired, too, but he can't possibly acknowledge such a thing. He's the headmaster. He is obliged to feel and to see that it all matters. The big game must be big. Maybe it is big, and I am too diminished to see it. That's what's wrong with me, Little Book, no big game on my schedule. Just tests.

John misses me. He's never quite right when he's by himself. But he's right to be there, me here. He may crash around a bit, fidget around the house, but in the office he'll be blessedly, savingly on task. He will phone and scribble, meet and plan. People will present wonderful and vexing knots for him to untie. Until he's home again, with his drink in the study, he'll be fine. Poor John, sweet love, sweet lover.

If I weren't an ailing, pallid old coot behind the screens, I would get out on the dock and empty the dinghy of last night's rain, paddle out to the Valmar and pump out her bilge, so that Fred and Valerie will know we've done Our Part when they come up this weekend to cruise. Fact is the very thought of padding down the hill to the dock and trying to turn that nine-ton dory on its side makes me shuffle toward the bed. For one thing that's no kind of dinghy to have. Why couldn't we have one of those weightless little white ones with the optional sailing gear for the putative grandchildren? Fred, however, insisted on a hulk of a craft rivaling the Valmar itself for size and heaviness. Possibly he was motivated by boyhood visions of himself in *Captains Courageous.* The dory in fairness would be a good vessel from which to harpoon blue whales, but as a dinghy to ferry us (ferry to dinghy us?) fifty yards between mooring and dock it is a mistaken choice. Nobody is comfortable plying its great oaken oars. Personally, I get almost no purchase on the water line when, even seated on a cushion, the oar handles meet me at the level of my forehead. Under the legitimate cover of ill health, I will let the dinghy become a bathtub of rainwater. Perhaps all the horrible pincher bugs will abandon ship. Over to you, Fred.

Afternoon, a long one. The day refuses to improve. Maybe a little fire will roast away the damp. Later. Tea, toast , and jam, which I thought might make a needed break from tinned tuna poached in water. Didn't do the trick, although perhaps not the jam's fault. So, so strange to will a mouthful of food along its dry descent. I must return to broth. Good old salty broth still seems to belong in my mouth.

Some nice busy Handel things on the little black Sony will liven things up a bit. Why does music sound so good in this cottage and so muted and ordinary on our sleek and reputedly excellent stereo in the school house? Also, how can such pure and finely differentiated sound come from the three little tiers of this Sony? John says it cost about a hundred dollars. It plays discs, it plays tapes, it makes a radio, and its mysterious little ruby light is always on. In the dark it's like an ancient eye, and I feel in those hours that the Sony knows me.

A perfect afternoon you would think (*do* you think, Little Book? If so, for God's sake, speak up!) for an x-word puzzle, but once again the *NY Times* lets me down. The only undone puzzles are Tuesday's and Sunday's which I'm saving for the unbearable, semi-naked intervals between Dr. K's tests. Even with plodding deliberation and exquisite penmanship, the Tuesday puzzle went down in 21 minutes. I am saddened anew remembering the purer puzzles of yore. Those were the days, when a puzzle was a puzzle. Now airplane magazine puzzles are cleverer. And who needs all the brand names and pop group references? What's wrong with freezing topical awareness at the point where the name of FDR's dog and "Only a paper____" come readily to a puzzlist's lips? So sad to have to pen in (again) "Pop singer John"—always Elton. I wouldn't mind so much if I hadn't seen Elton John once on some sort of television celebration. Very disturbing—a kind of sad and beefy accountant, uncomfortable at the piano bench, wearing peculiar glasses with lenses framed in heart-shaped plastic. Very, very off-putting. I believe there is something deeply wrong with pop singer John. But worse, today's clue "Lexicographer's bane" yielded "neologism." Why? Why would a neologism be a lexicographer's bane? If I were a lexicographer, a neologism would be my delight, my lexigraphic reason for being. I suppose I could write a letter of complaint to the puzzle editor at the *Times* since, after just twenty-one minutes, I have plenty of time, but I am sure his desk is spilling over with such letters. As Flower the skunk said to Bambi (or was it, I think, to Thumper?) if you don't have anything nice to say, don't say anything at all. Good advice, Little Book, but if I took it then where would you and I be? Maybe both of us still virgins. Darkness coming and, if I can stir, a fire. So long, B. I love you.

August 30

More soup and gloom. Temperature on rising 99.5°. Is this possibly not another day at all but yesterday again, seeking to improve?

"Both of us still virgins," I see I wrote. So queer to feel that even now, in apparent ruin sitting in the internal murk of a cottage on a cape where the sun is past shining, I still feel a recent virgin. Oh, Little Book, I remember it, virginity. I remember the waiting, waiting with all my might.

So odd, but also somehow inevitable, that God would send me not the angular Robert Lowell who, trembling with nicotine and God knows what demons, thrilled my every cell as I sat like an adoring idiot in his poetry seminar, but the less glamorously tortured Philip Lowenthal.

Poor soul. In a pitiful way I wanted to make Philip Lowenthal into Robert Lowell. No mean feat, although Philip wore the same dark-rimmed glasses. Philip was very,

very smart, monstrously bookish really, when I think back on him. What I didn't fully get then, although I felt it enormously, was that Philip's smartness and desperate intellectual affectations were his way of being afraid. What were you so afraid of, Philip? I never knew, never thought to find out. Did you ever find out?

What I did find out and what finally confirmed that Philip Lowenthal and I must not share a future was that he liked me because he thought I was just like him. He liked me best when he thought I was very, very smart. He wanted us to be talky, creepy, acutely critical partners in knowing more than anybody else. He would go into nervous ecstasy whenever somebody's facts were wrong or their reasoning was haywire. He was always reaching for a larger, often preposterous, context into which to put the most ordinary thoughts, as if establishing context put you above context—and then you win. At Radcliffe, Valerie thought Philip was hilarious, which actually miffed me. If he was so hilarious, why didn't I know it? Once during a no doubt insufferable interlude with Philip and me in the bar of the Wursthaus—probably discussing where we would meet later for dinner and spend almost no money and, because they are so helpful in such deliberations, Rilke, Freud, Reich, Spinoza, and Pascal—Val got up to leave and told Philip: "I'm going over to the Coop bookstore to find a whole bunch of books you've never even heard of." I thought this was funny. Philip couldn't see the joke. Very transparently he was rattled that someone could go off, even someone like Val, and, by sheer whim and purchase, acquire books he had not heard of. *What did she mean by that?* Philip asked me with amazing denseness. It's a compliment, I assured him in utter dishonesty.

Although he didn't know it, Philip didn't need me, but he did need me to be like him. But I wasn't, and he never could get used to that. It rather terrified him if I loafed or let someone's silly opinion or enthusiasm go—or, far more outrageous for him, when I agreed with something fatuous because a beautiful person said it. What I wanted, if I had paused to sort it out and name it, was for Harvard and Cambridge and art and the pulse of the hour to sweep me away on some kind of adventure. For Robert Lowell to look over his horned rims into my unbatting eyes and say, *Would you please read your poem again, Miss Chasin*—and to start making plans about me? Philip expected, because he was so fundamentally frightened and I was presumably so much like him, that I must be similarly afraid. But I wasn't. However I appeared at the time (how did I appear? Radcliffe photos show sharp nose, sharp chin, bangs and straight hair, mischief in the eyes), I was not afraid. I was the opposite of afraid. I wanted someone to take me and my virginity away. I always thought one of those dashing and wealthy and fairly stupid Porcellian boys might improbably, given Philip stationed anxiously and hypercritically at my elbow, take me away. But in the event (perfect phrase!) it was tortured Lowenthal. He wasn't actually bad looking. Nice, almost pretty bones in his face, but those dark eyes and his worried mouth were never at rest. He exuded no confidence. He was fussy and needy, and he adored me. What a salvation that even daring couples didn't live together in Cambridge of that era. Philip would have lived with me. Thank you, God. I would not have been alone even brushing my teeth or sleeping in late or looking in the mirror. Oh, Philip—what did you feel like? How did you smell? He could fuss for an eternity about which dreary restaurant to go to, about the exact cost of horrible ordinary things, of each kind of beer, of a dish of ice cream, of the T versus a cab on a rainy night. All the while, Philip Lowenthal, you could have kissed and fondled me into a lather in the darkened pews of Memorial Church, thoughtfully, I felt, left open in the evenings for such ardor or even prayer. You could have whisked me arm in arm to the banks of the Charles and, with very little discussion, ravished me on the damp grass. Ravished. That's what I wanted, to be ravished, to be rapt, not, I think, to be raped, but something rather close to that, to be taken in some all new unanswerable way, to have it over with, to have it begin.

When, in the event, it happened, in March at Blue Hill on the floor of the boathouse to which we had furtively sneaked in Frank Greeve's bulbous Buick, I was not rapt. I was—grimly methodical. The fog and the

21

damp chilled me all the way inside my vertebrae, my knees, my fingers, my skull. Philip had clearly read no books, seen no films. "Meg," he asked me, outrageously, "Are you sure?" Awful, awful Philip. I was sure, absolutely sure: sure that the only thing more deadeningly arduous than evoking intercourse from him was to return to Cambridge having failed either to try or execute the operation. My humor, though lying way low, did not abandon me, and I must have been more excited than I am able to recall right now, but for what memory is worth, my deflowering was about as satisfying as a bowl of dry cereal. Due to the cold and to Philip's desperate modesty, we managed the preliminaries and even, finally, penetration without really undressing at all. When, very quickly, Philip was finished, I was relieved and grateful. Sexual connection, about which I had not yet one vivid clue, seemed now at least possible. I had done it, technically. I was on my way, which seemed to grant a kind of permission to disengage myself from Philip Lowenthal and to get as far away from him as I could.

Funny how in hindsight I don't think of him more fondly. He was my first youthful acquaintance to die. Stomach cancer. If possible, I think of him less warmly than ever—maybe it's my malaise, but I don't think so. I think Philip Lowenthal was a parasite. His timidity was not from primal wounds but from narcissism, a despicable dread of giving himself up and away. He left less life than he found. He made no love and thus failed to matter. When I think of him now, I can see only horn-rimmed glasses and his clothes, his mist-frizzed pea coat and our blanket on the weathered boards of the boat house floor.

Has this grim recollection come to visit me, or have I dredged it up myself as a suitable experience onto which to project my own loveless (and appetite-less) condition? I hope not, yet fear so.

Darkening now. Smoky grey shadows on the water outside, still and oily. I won't pretend to eat supper. Some tea with honey, Brahms. I'll huddle under the afghan and watch a fire. Call John before ten. Temperature 99.5°. Help me to do better tomorrow, Little Book.

August 31

Awoke to pure azure above the dark pines. Felt a little leap of hope, raised my head. But nope. Soot behind the eyes, the awful tense little hum behind my breast bone. Pee seems thick or not quite right, unless I'm imagining things. Temperature 100. I am wrong, all wrong. Not the way I feel, but knowing the wrongness, left a hard ball of dread in my guts. Juice, water, tea with honey. By mid-morning fear begins to dissolve.

Called Dr. K. to report my flat, unacceptable condition. He is concerned—sweet—and says he will try to get my tests moved up from the 7th to the 4th. Now, for some reason, this sounds like a good idea. Yes, let's *do* something to this malaise. Let's poke it, suck out samples, fry it with x-rays. Let's hurt the bugger back.

Called John to say about the tests change and ask him, breezily, not to come down. Dear love, his anxious witness only amplifies my own. I tell him I'm fine. I joke about my diet of canned tuna. I blather on about putative days on boats, the bird feeder, convey the impression I'm actually out in the weather. It's my good luck that J. is actually distracted. T.H., a young and very goofy math teacher has broken his contract and, on the brink of the term, bolted. This kind of thing always amazes J. I understand it perfectly. J., believing all human beings are endowed at birth with a capacity for empathy and a working forebrain, cannot understand how someone can Let Down the Side, knowing the trouble it causes others. I understand it perfectly. That very fact, the impending reality of a world, Wells School, where one must never Let Down the Side, feels stifling, feels an intolerable prison to a certain kind of soul. Of course they bolt. It could be a matter of spiritual life or death. What a world. We have to negate things in order to live; passionate affirmation blinds and ultimately kills us. But poor J. Where in late August do you find a mathematician who can keep the rascals of Wells in line? What such person is idling around, open to an invitation to descend into the den of a boys' boarding school in nether Connecticut? Oddly, this is the kind of pebble J. seems to like in his shoe. He actually finds such people.

I should not be mean about Wells. Wells has been sweet to me. The whole socio-economic complex has been sweet to me, provided me with houses full of rooms, things to eat, periodically sent me careering around the globe. Great libraries amass books for me to read. I am squired to heartbreakingly beautiful plays and concerts. I have been asked to do virtually no work. No one infringes on my liberties. I have never felt compelled to answer a phone. No one makes me entertain deadening people in my home simply because they insist on entertaining me. I have been free. I can go outside, or not, or could until my maker threw this grey and raspy blanket of flu over my head.

I must take pains to remember, Little Book, that I have been dealt a fabulous hand. Inwardly and outwardly I have probed and sometimes flown off where no one could ever have imagined. For no good reason, some people have loved me. I have loved them back. J., Brian. I awake from first memory into a great, cosmic conversation, still coming, still going, even through the static and gloom of this bug.

Chicken broth, toast, and a sent-from-heaven, deeper-than-deep nap. Awoke in a light, pleasant sweat. Temperature a shade under 99°. Ta-dah!

This music, Brahms again, is just about perfect. Sun's down, the sky is still glass-blue. A chill in the house, but there are fixings for at least a few more fires. It's time to clean up this joint. Night-night, b.

September 1

Meg Greeve, the dynamo.

Perhaps the answer all along was to spring out of bed like a robot, stir the stumps, and get on with it. In just a single sunny Cape Cod day she changed the bed, laundered sickness and self-pity out of the sheets and towels. Scoured tub and tiles. Pine soap in the pine air.

Motored into E. Sandwich, replenished cleansers, toothpaste, shampoo, soup supply. Dew-daubed blueberries and surreally gorgeous tomatoes stand ready on the counter.

Swept pine debris from deck and stoop.

Strode down to the dock, bailed the swollen dory with a milk carton till it became thinkable to haul her up onto the float, upend and empty her of weeks' accumulated rain and muck. Gallons of guilt slopped over the gunwales as I stood winded and righteous in my sopping sneakers. It was good to greet the gulls again. Felt rather an old gull myself.

No sooner was the deed done than Val and Frank appeared in their jeep. Lemonade on the sunny deck, and the hearty recluse Meg helped them stow groceries and booze on the Valmar, Frank clearly itching to get off, Val somehow conveying a desire to linger. Poor Val. There's no loneliness like loneliness in a boat. I know V.'s got clubby chums back in Tarrytown, but we go back. We were soul sisters before turning into—shudder to say it—mature women, fixed and finished selves. Even more than I, she likes to stop the action, sink back into the unsorted-out haze of our Radcliffe time, pose the old questions, as if there were other answers. Such a sad look from the stern— for herself or for me?—as they motored off toward the harbor mouth.

Chicken broth, tuna and buttered toast. While probably not good for me, a longish glass of Chardonnay, although I was stupefyingly tired already. My bug sends off clear aversive signals about alcohol, and the wine was acidy on my tongue, but the hoped-for agreeable effect followed: a restful, disconnected lightheadedness. Hovering a little above myself, I turned back clean, ironed sheets.

Temperature just under 100. Who cares. Just buttery light from the bedside lamp. Outside, the faint slosh of waves against the float, distant peepers, crickets. My fingers curled around the pen look bony and sharp, an old person's claw. Do we care, Little Book?

September 3

Fair sky again and coolness from the N.W., but no good at the Greeve interior. Temperature 99.5°. No appetite, stomach clenched and sour-feeling.

J. called just before noon, annoyed with the service, especially the sermon at St. James, apparently on the theme of strength through acknowledging one's hopeless weakness. J. said all that came through was the hopelessness and weakness. J. meant to be amusing, I think, but the point unsettled me a good deal. We chatted about Val and Frank. J. asked me if I wished we had joined them on their cruise. He knew I would say no, and I wondered what he felt, whether he was disappointed. Later, after he had hung up, I went very low realizing I would never want to cruise again—with Val or Frank or anybody. All of that is not only physically unimaginable for me right now, I just know it is over. Forgive me, b., but this afternoon everything feels as if it's about to be over. Maybe it's the dread of tomorrow's tests, but I am afraid it's beyond that. I honestly don't know whether I really care about the tests. It would be nice if this punk, heavy feeling would lift, but nothing inside me wants to raise sail and catch the wind to Menemsha Bight—not one time, not ever. Nor can I imagine the mouse-stirrings of sexual feeling, the flickers and flashes of light from my writers, none of the blessed things. This is so sad, so strange. It is crying without convulsion, without tears, without affect. Whatever is grieving here, it is not my body. Oh God help me.

A pint of cool water. Tea with honey.

I have pulled collected poems of Edna St. V. Millay from the shelf. Long time no see, E. So tired, bone tired not sleepy, I couldn't make myself turn back the cover. I lay back and remembered Edna, or my Radcliffe dream of her. I remember, especially after hearing a recording of her reading, falling in love with her and with the idea of her. Airy as a hummingbird, but also somehow substantial and urgent, E. was so juicy, so sexy to me. Startled, wounded, but O.K., she was, long before Josephine Baker or Frieda Kahlo or all of these Madonnas, right out there, indomitable and doomed at the same time.

> We were very tired, we were very merry
> As we rode back and forth all night on the ferry.

Oh, Edna St. Vincent Millay, where did you go? The plan, once, was to make you mine. No matter how many

30

lucid critics and biographers you had already, you were going to be mine. The secret was that you—that is, you as I held you—were really me, and that in finding and telling you, I was going to find and tell me. I was the type. I pictured myself, outwardly eloquent and fastidious, opening up your beautiful, incautious soul (my incautious soul) to the world. My readers would be drawn to you, and like all readers of great biographers would be baffled going back to the lifeless documents of your life and to your poems, failing to find the thrilling sparks they felt in my life of you. They would fail because you were the occasion for the thrilling sparks, but they were my sparks. Perhaps I should have done it. Elsewhere in nature creatures are given life—and in a way create life—by infesting the being of another. Oh my God, oh my Edna, I was alive then. I was ready, I was trembling in anticipation. God, the power of that, even the memory. Perky bird-beaked Meg Chasin was free love, was Nietzsche with a womb. I was in my heart so sun burnt, so far beyond convention that I felt no need whatsoever to strike an unconventional pose. When I needed to speak as Aphrodite, Edna would speak on my behalf.

So sleepy, never did open the book. Tests tomorrow. I will be put to the test.

September 4,5

Oh, Little Book. Abandoned, shut fast in my bag, you were there yesterday, but you can't know. I thought, I hoped there would be long stretches of sitting/waiting during which I could scrawl my stories and jokes about the Tests, but the hospital folks had other things in mind for me. Medical idiot that I am, I was expecting the terrors and indignities to be lightened by the physical presence and simian charms of Dr. Karipides, but of course he wasn't even there. It had not even dawned on me that he wouldn't do the tests. Specialists do the tests—actually not. Sad-looking, beaten men in late middle years—the specialists—talk to you for about a minute and a half. With amazing, depressing economy, they tell you what's going to happen to you and why and express a clear but unstated hope that you won't ask them any questions. The tests themselves are performed by Amazonian young women with lesser, different kinds of medical credentials. The unvarying manic cheerfulness of the girl technicians strikes me as a sustained, largely unconscious apology for everything that is happening. Thank God Dr. K. didn't give me a clue about what they were going to do.

Best line of the day was from the technician preparing me for the coloscopy. "Mrs. Greeve, I should tell you that some patients find this procedure unpleasant." *Unpleasant.* This from the profession that calls the excruciating pains of child birth "contractions." And yes, Miss, I must now count myself among that list of patients who found the coloscopic procedure unpleasant. Moreover, I would be fascinated to meet someone who found the insertion of something that feels like pinking sheers up one's bum and the subsequent snipping away "pleasant," or even ho-hum. Poor bum, already insulted lewdly by an early a.m. enema, followed by inquiries from more than a few rubber-gloved fingers.

No more tests for me, Little Book. I'll take the fever and the tuna. The blood-letting now frightens me less, since they've done so much of it, but it still makes me mad. The damn needle burns, burns the whole time it's in there, as box after plastic box is filled up—so much of it! I've never liked thinking of myself as pump and con-duits of purple-black blood. I know God wants it to stay inside of us. A nice person hates to see it.

Another lulu: "you might get a funny taste in your mouth."

This before I was excruciatingly injected with some

kind of dye that the MRI scanners are supposed to watch as it seeps through your bloodstream. They inject you in the crook of your arm, and suddenly, as if spewing out of your tonsils there is a mouth full of something like powdered aluminum and Pepto Bismol. I can still taste it. I can now not imagine not tasting it. My tea, my chicken broth pass over a tongue saturated with metallic chalk.

Oh Meg, you silly old crone, carping and complaining. Here modern, high-tech medicine has gathered you into itself for the better part of a whole day. Modern insurers have treated you to thousands of dollars worth of advances. All you had to do was point your Toyota in the direction of the facility. Think how smiley and clean those women technicians were on their bouncy-soled athletic shoes. And what about the x-rays? You can't complain about x-rays. Quiet, quick, not one single intrusion up your bum or into a tired old vein. A second's buzz and thank you very much. For that matter, the scanning machine, after the shock of my aluminum frappe, was kind of an adventure. Very solicitously, the technical assistant seemed to assume a claustrophobic response on my part— maybe most people are. But not at all. I was actually in the mood to lie for a while perfectly still in a dark steel drawer. I believe I rather pulled myself together in there.

No, in the future I will approach these outings with a policy intact. Except maybe to prick my finger tip, they may take no more of my blood. Nor will buggery of any kind in any sanitized guise be permitted. By compensation, because I am reasonable and modern, they can scan and x-ray the hell out of me.

It is very strange what happens to you when you are being done one way or another all day in a hospital. It is all so finally and overwhelmingly about your body, about the biology and mechanics of your body, that your soul doesn't know what to do. The soul is utterly unaddressed by tests. It detaches from the body and is temporarily dumb. Maybe for this reason I honestly did not know, while I was being jabbed and dyed and zapped, how I felt. I forgot if I was sick, suspended the ability to tell. Also, in a way I am still trying to sort out, I feel as though the hospital—more accurately, the medical process—has gathered me up and into itself. It's not just that in their clinically vampirish way they have extracted my essences—blood, urine, stool, tissue from my deep interior—it feels that in giving myself up to them all day yesterday, however timidly, I had worshipped at their altars. I think the Latin *religare* in religion means *to bind*. I don't know if I like it, and I'm sure I never wanted it, but medicine and I are now bound. By Friday I should know what medicine makes of me. It'll be nice to get the verdict through the animal warmth of Dr. K. But whatever it is, book-y, don't let me forget the rest of me. Don't let me shrink into my diagnosis. My soul. Let's remember there's me in there.

J. helps. He loves me. His worry and smart questions were like a warm bath last night. Bless that good man's heart. He doesn't hear a beaky old bag of bones with limp hair; he hears Meg Greeve, a woman he loves. A whole, well woman, a woman in any case beyond her diagnosis. I love this man.

So, b., here's how it is. I have to give myself up to this now. I didn't will it to begin with, and I won't waste a second trying to will it away. Let's get beyond symptoms and my testy, squeamish concerns about them. What do you say, Little Book, you and me?

September 6

Actually slept deeply, awoke warm and moist with sweat. Temperature a little over 99°.

Lay in bed for an hour with the most pleasing reveries on "too bright flames." This morning all of them, or at least the idea of them, seem to be talking to me in the sweetest way. What did Romeo say of J.—"beauty too rich for use"? This morning it is nice, and not morbid, to think about beauty too rich for use. Nice to think about who qualifies as such a beauty. My Edna, of course, Mozart (at moments), John Keats (always), Thoreau, Rilke, Nathanael West, Gershwin, Sylvia Plath (at least for this morning). All burning too bright, all in that danger zone, letting themselves accelerate like hummingbirds, burning up, burning out.

I wonder if the Too Bright Flame card comes up for everyone? Did it come up for me? *Did* it? And did I pass? If it did, it was at or just after Cambridge. It was in my Edna/Rilke/Nietzsche thrall. And Wilhelm Reich! I almost forgot Wilhelm Reich! Talk about Too Bright Flames! Oh, my God, Reich—how did I get on to him in the first place? He can't have come within miles of a syllabus. It must have been Philip, of course it was. Philip dismissing Reich as Freud gone wrong. I remember the thrill of deciding Reich was Freud gone right, gone all the way. I don't really know whether I came to this reading honestly, or whether I just wanted it to be the case. I'm sure I wanted to knock Philip for a loop, but it was more than that. Reich used to thrill me.

What was it? And where are my Reich books? Did I even keep them? I think so. Think I see them on a low, dim shelf in the T.V. room at School House. I'd kill for them right now. What was it? It must have been W.R.'s flat out, brave look at the body. He wasn't afraid of it, wasn't afraid to look. He knew, thanks to his own wretched story, how before thought and word, the body slams shut, contracts its muscular armor to ward off blows. Diaphragm, stomach, womb—we clench and close in terror before we ever take much of anything in or let much of anything out. We grow warily into consciousness as shallow breathers, picky eaters, sexual ghosts. The ideological props follow—shame at what should evoke wonder, guilt about even an intimation of ecstasy, analysis and negation where there should be communion and booming affirmation. Cowardice and compliance set up as proper conduct. All of it is held in place, at a devastating psychic and physical price, by tacitly held repressions. Clenched and armored in our collective repression, modern man and woman make their tentative anxious way. Truth tellers are anomalies, and given the terrifying and repellent tone of the truths they tell, we marginalize them. Let them be immolated in their own discovered fire. We told them so, after all. Maybe we will peer at their sanitized and stylized legacies through art, a medium, while itself annoyingly volatile, at a good remove from one's own diaphragm, stomach, womb.

Wilhelm Reich. Where did you go? What an unlikely saint to appear suddenly on the coast of Maine. Pinched and driven, garlic-breathed, at a glance no fun. You conveyed the warmth of Lenin, the empathic sweetness of Brecht, the social ease of Solzhenitsyn. At the time I realized that to understand you and accept you, I had to accept, without averting my eyes or breathing through my mouth, the fetid chaos of my nihilist friends' unspeakable rooms and flats. I had to will the acceptance of and assign a welcome place to unlovely bodies. Reich wanted me to look straight ahead at everything. The thing I needed most to look straight ahead at and I suppose, in a deep way, wanted most to look straight ahead at was sex. Here, besides being rapt, I stood utterly alone. Certainly no girl, no woman of my acquaintance shared or wanted to consider any of this. Not Val certainly, and certainly not Philip. Reichean thinking I see now was a good way to punch Philip in the nose, clear him off my horizon. But to go after and into Reich—that is, *my* Reich, which may have been as idiosyncratic as my Edna St. V. Millay—I would have to go right into sex, go "all the way."

Reich is terrific on sex, on the actual animal act. Not to sound too much like my late-twentieth-century sisters, I have to add that old W.R. was way better about man sex than woman sex. But he got everything right, I think, about straight ahead coital orgasm. Which happens to be, in this world we have settled for, an erotic *rara avis*. But Reich let you know he knew. He charted the trajectory of spark, frenzy, release, oblivion. He was specially good on oblivion, the reabsorbtion into the primal dark, the ultimate rest. No one else was saying this. No one else was talking about a sleep deeper than fucking. Poor W.R., he knew—everybody in the thrall of deep sex knows—that orgasm isn't a localized spill, a mere "release of tension." In deep orgasmic release we come ecstatically into tune with higher frequencies. Orgasmic partners don't *do it* to each other, nor do they *get off* separately. Or maybe they do both things, but the deeper, realer fact is that for an instant they join a bigger, cosmic orgasm. This is the experience for which we have no words, except terrible words. This is what we wordlessly affirm with every cell of ourselves deep in our knowing. How sadly, comically touching that W.R. set out to harness the force itself in his clunky Box and other contraptions. But he did that prior great thing. He figured out more honestly than Freud how fear and pain can shut down our bodies and preoccupy our souls. He knew how to fix that, how to touch, to restore breath, to rekindle the sacred back to full fire. He didn't need to fabricate noble savages and unspoiled Samoans to make his point. Oh, W.R., why couldn't you have been a little beautiful? What if you had been funny? Or patient or artful? W.R., you or somebody like you could have helped the whole human race to unfurl in erotic delight. What if you had been reasonable and eloquent? Who really opposes ecstasy? Think of it—the remedy immediately at hand and economically feasible. Why do only tortured charlatans and barely awake adolescents carry the banner? Who has allowed the sexual impulse to be gloriously out only if handcuffed to sadism and self-loathing? The sleazification of sex is an unearned acknowledgment, a sheer projection of every deadening fear of it. W.R., you were great and true, and then you let yourself be reduced to a clown. Or is it that real sex reduces anybody to a clown? There was that time, that actual time, when I would have proudly been a clown. Why wasn't I braver? Is that the path my Too Bright Flames have been lighting for me today?

Temperature down a bit. Tea with honey, broth, tuna on buttered toast. It tastes a bit. Sex, even missing it, is so good for you. Good night, b.

September 7

Little continuous sleep. Arose feeling dry, weak, no energy. Then the terrible call.

Dr. Karipides, himself no less, rang up to say most of the tests were ready and that I should come to see him tomorrow a.m. at his office in Falmouth. I had already determined his voice was funny before he added the awful "and it would be a good idea of your husband could join us." Then of course I was obliged to ask why, to which Dr. K. was predictably and professionally maddening. "The tests raise some concerns," he said. "We may have to begin thinking about some decisions." Oh for God's sake, I told him, tell me what I've got. He couldn't, or wouldn't. "Not everything is clear," was the polite evasion. Does Dr. K. have any idea what kind of day he has created for me? Could he possibly believe that we who ail are comforted by the language of Tests revealing Concerns which require Decisions—when Tests mean snipping off bits of you, sucking out your blood, dying it

42

blue, Concerns are malignant indications of your death, and Decisions are which grim bus to the terminal. "You're not going to tell me the bad news, are you?" I said, not very generously, to Dr. K. He told me it would be better to wait and he would know more tomorrow. Then he asked me how I was feeling.

Called J. with the news, hating to bring him low, feeling like an angry, slippery Dr. K. myself as I failed to supply a single concrete fact of the reassurance I know he needs. I mouth "concerns" and "decisions" and "know more tomorrow" with a hurt lack of conviction that J. rightly reads as Worst Case Coming. I could hear his voice go thin, his loss of pace, his tension amplifying my own. I could see it all, leaving "instructions" for his office and staff, the grim, hasty packing, shutting the door of the dim and empty house behind him. He would drive off from Wells blanched in summer sunlight. He would pass distractedly the fall athletes on the practice fields, not really hearing the yelps and heys. He would never let himself resent their incongruous, oblivious vitality and health. He will be four and a half hours coming to me, two of them through late summer Cape traffic. He will idle, inch along the clutter and heat. He will let Worst Cases and, who knows, perhaps even Best Cases, compare themselves in his head. He will prepare. He will prepare his words and questions for me. He will prepare for the Concerns and for the Decisions. Poor, lonely, beaten J. He will take this on. He will take me on. There is no way I can spare him this. I'm going to clean up Little House, set out some flowers. It is good August hot today, and the sun is beating down on the deck. J. will arrive to find his faithful gull sitting in the sun, looking out to sea.

Last peach-tinted afternoon light on the deck and— shunk, shoonk—the station wagon's doors are shut and there is the willowy old headmaster ambling up the path, a boy's canvas duffle bag strapped over his shoulder. He is still tanned, looks a little weary.

"Hey, Miss Chasin," he calls up to me. "You don't look so bad."

I know, I say, I was just bored and wanted some company. As we held each other, he started kneading my boney back and asked me if I was disappearing. Like Echo, I told him, Echo pining for Narcissus. J. seemed, though I didn't tell him, absolutely massive, all bone and sinew.

We had white wine on the deck. Nice. I had to tell J. the supper options were tuna with tomato or tuna without tomato. He asked me if I wanted to go out, and I felt an all-body aversion, reminding me sickeningly of Concerns. I am not right. I can't imagine sitting through the eternity of a restaurant meal. We decide J. will run out to Sandwich Center for some provisions and a lobster roll for himself. We light a candle on the kitchen table. A second glass of wine. Head now about eighteen inches above my chalky malaise. Broth and toast for me. J.'s lobster roll looks about the size of a live rabbit. He eats it all. Tea. A very nice time, and I marvel at not wanting him sooner. It is good, deep, safe to be close to J. I am aware of his hip near my hip at the counter. His voice, apart from any words, deepens me. Oh, I love this craggy man. I am so lucky.

In bed J. reads for only a minute, turns out the light on his side. He holds me and asks if I'm all right. I tell him I want to get on with it, on to whatever. As I say it, I realize I do. For the first time since I knew I was good and sick, I do.

Tonight, because J. is here, huge and warm and sleeping at my side, I can think about dying. I have to get it straight, think through how it might happen—how it will happen. Worst Case. Either they're going to want to cut something unspeakable out of me, then scorch my system with killer chemicals or else they will decide what's gone wrong is the whole system, in which case it'll be only chemicals. That is a certain awfulness. It will be either temporary or it will be fatal. Now, let's look at fatal. I'll get flatter, duller. In worst flu, I can't imagine extending my arm to the night table to pick up a glass or turn off the light. I lie still and dully agitated. I have to pee, but can't begin to mobilize the enormity of the exertion necessary to rise and walk. With flu, inertia and surrender and waiting have always done the trick. When we've moved from Concerns to Decision, waiting and surrender will lead to death. Now, that part. Death coming, and I am sick and tired and resigned to it. The body, or most of it, moronically carries out the old instructions. Heart flub-flubbing audibly beneath my breast bone, sick baby gruel passing through my bowels, hair (if any) oilier each day, fingernails irrelevantly growing. And pain. I've got to get real about pain. Bearing pain has not been a strength. I don't even do well with malaise. I invent pains, imagine them. So, let's say the real thing sets in, grinding, seizing me in waves, like being burned at the stake. Say it's cancer, the kind that eats up tissue, bears on nerves, sears me like hot knives running the length of my bones. There are pain medicines, deep narcotics. Do they always work, are they sometimes not enough? Very bad to die in pain, to pass on in visible agony. This would be demoralizing and an unfair burden for J. What else? I'm sure there are terrors I have no idea about. I wish I could remember which grim Russian said that each of us dies completely alone, no sharing or lightening this passage. God, help me. Help me to do this as well as I can. Please let this be my best gift to J. Let my love rise to this. Courage and judgment, please.

Very late—I am a little afraid to stop scribbling, give up this inky thread of control. Darkness beckons, if not sleep. We have been Tested, book-y. Hold on tight.

September 9

As we thought, book-y, as we thought.

It appears that I am rotten through and through. But haven't we, at moments, in our heart of hearts, known this all along? The new killer word—perfect—is "involved" as in lungs are involved, esophagus and stomach are involved. Oh, b., so many parts of me are involved. Treacherous, shameful parts. Damn them for their infidelity, their slovenly willingness to become involved. Are you happy now, ileum? Lung? You will soon see it doesn't pay to get involved.

"Let me show you what we're dealing with," says Dr. K. uncomfortably. Ghostly x-rays and scans are illuminated from behind to show fuzzy little blurs along the margins of, or deep within, what I must accept on faith are very internal organs. So that's what kills you—vagueness, poor definition. I am blanking on the exact name of my culprit—melanoma, carcinoma, Pamplona—they all sound to me like Caribbean fruits or ranges of the Sierras.

I will get it tomorrow—if that's possible on a Saturday. I want to know my -*noma*, involver of my organs, look the bugger in the eye. It's funny that now I have such tender feelings for my immune system, or whatever uninvolved part of me is registering the weak/achy/insulted reaction to my pathology. It's amazing that at the brute biological level, at the level of virus and antibody, the body can report wrongness in such a nuanced, darkly elegant way. If we're not careful we get angry at and want to annihilate the faithful messengers, the "symptoms." Poor babies.

As for my deadly -*noma*, Dr. K. suggested that I take my bundle of hopeless involvements A.S.A.P. to Mass. General in Boston for treatment. Slightly more in range of Wells. I almost wrote "home." It sounds like a few punishing rounds of chemotherapy. Even though it's Mass. General's job to tell me in full detail, Dr. K. pretty much assured me that the treatment will nauseate, desiccate, and depilate me within an inch of my waning life. The idea is to undergo a week's "course" of the chemicals, suffer, then, if and when one is able to resume an upright position, step up for another "course." Looks like two or three courses for me. I guess the very superficial good news is that there will be no surgical invasions and mutilations—I'm too involved. Not wanting to make Dr. K. uncomfortable, I nevertheless had to ask him whether someone in my condition ever got better. It would depend on my response to the chemicals, Dr. K. said very evenly. Then: "it happens." Good enough for me. My return to health is at least as likely as the parting of the Red sea, the virgin birth, stigmata, winning the lotto.

Probably a delayed reaction, but I didn't feel frightened or overwhelmed getting the verdict from Dr. K., or even on the ride home. Bless J.'s heart. His first words to me: "so what do we think?" We didn't think much. It was such a relief. I did fall apart a bit when we got home to Little House. It was on the deck while J. was unlocking the door. I happened to look out over the harbor and I caught sight of a wind-surfer, the words were suddenly out of my mouth: *we have to find Brian.* It was a strange, outraged feeling. What have I been *doing*, forgetting him, eclipsing him? Have I become more involved in my deadly -*nomas* than with my living son? Truth is, I haven't thought about Brian for days, not even as a great deep absence. I don't think I have ever done that before. I forgot him.

Remembering undid me, that horrible, almost peristaltic cramping and convulsing, a braying animal grief forced up and out into the audible air. Poor J. I could not stop the flow of images; Brian hunched over the breakfast counter, his beautiful, beautiful shoulders straining the tattered ruins of a sweater, his thoughtful, sleepy eyes. I could see him hoisting his own bean pole length up onto the sail board, stepping windward of the sail, bowing back from the billowing sheet and taking soundless flight.

Dark stick against electric blue sail; soon an iridescent feather flickering far across the bay. Where are you, Brian Greeve, my brooding heart? I see you ambling down an ancient beach, ambling away from me. I see you alone, alone in a café, alone in a rail carriage. All alone, all alone. I hope you think about us sometimes, even if they are flat and loveless thoughts. I hope I am a *presence* in you, just as you are forever a presence in me.

Brian, Brian, Brian! Come here. I need you to know this new dark thing, this change, this difference. You must not read it in a letter. You must not open this squeaky door one day, or God forbid reenter the drills and bells of Wells, and learn that I have gone. You must not be startled by that particular silence. There has been too much silence with us, boy-o. Come up, come out, come here. I want to see your slow smile. I want to see that clown spot of high color that glowed into being when you were about to laugh. You know you could break through this time. If you were a presence at my passing, you could be set free. You could see, maybe even grieve at the finitude of me, and thus of us, after all. Maybe it would be like Dorothy watching the Wicked Witch of the West melt into harmlessness at last. I will melt for you, boy-o. I will drink my chemo elixir with a full heart if you will come home to me this once. Please God, please. I have believed in the efficacy of prayer. I have believed, actually felt, my desire changing every infinitesimal particle between myself and the object of my desire. This day, this night, and for as long as I can transmit, I will beam this appeal out over the sea and into the all. Switch on your receiver, beloved boy.

J. drove out to Sandwich for more provisions. We've decided to isolate ourselves for a day or two before Wells and chemo, our respective treatments. Hard not to, it's so crystalline beautiful. John brings back an already roasted chicken from the Stop 'n Shop, and a few tender scraps of it taste rather good on my buttered toast. Chilled Chardonnay is nice too. So sweet, so right being here with J. "A day or two" feels as if it could spread itself languorously out over all the time in the world. Maybe it will.

J. washes up. He was once again very hungry, and I can sense his feeling that this is somehow in bad taste, so he resorts to very *slowly* eating everything in sight. It bewilders him that he makes me laugh. With no clear need for one, we light a fire, which is very nice. Try T.V., but it is, as usual, unviewable. Where did this taste for the gritty doings of urban police stations and hospitals come from? I was just in a hospital, and it conveyed only the usual antiseptic gloom. The T.V. hospitals operate as if a bomb has just gone off in the next room. Surely no real person wheeled into a T.V. hospital on one of those flying gurneys attended by ten or twelve barking physicians, infusions, extractions, oxygen being applied on the run, would survive for fifteen minutes. Why this hunger for the frenetic, the pitch of desperation? The counterpoint scenes to the cyclones of medical intervention seem always to be rather seamy sexual come-ons across the various gradations of practitioner. The men are obviously too beleaguered with emergency to brush up and shave; they wear throw-away grunge clothes beneath their green hospital issue. The women are rather fetching in a blowsy carthy way. The hospital shows and even the police shows succeed in building a promising climate for sex; against so much desperate trauma and furious interventions, it would be prissy to stand by convention. Raise the arms, peel out of that tee shirt, let her rip. Might I sense any of this in the course of my chemo? I shall report faithfully.

We try again at news time. Much better. Something about the weirdly lobotomized attitude of the "anchors"—no matter in what outpost of the English speaking teleworld—makes the late-night news the same, and yet for me riveting. Today's weather, uniformly glass blue and warm all day, was, for the Boston meteorologist, dizzyingly dynamic and complex. In Hyannis, sadly, a baby whale came up onto the beach. Earnest hands were marshaled to tow it out to deep water, but it drifted sickly back and died. A house and garage burned down due to a faulty gas barbecue. The occupants appeared to be startled, grateful to be spared. The "amusing" story at the end was that a beloved old homeless Portuguese in New Bedford was offered what a benefactor believed was a nice home, which was declined. "And that's the news at eleven." Shuffle mock documents, exchange mock banter, up theme (Berlioz), up spiraling logos. Off, off!

Oh, the quiet. Embers, my warm and comfy J. One swallow of warming Chardonnay. Crickets carry me away.

You are a good friend to me today, b.

September 10

New day, b. Something feels important.

Timelessly, gloriously fresh green and blue out on our deck. The morning sun feels a bit like a clout on your white pages, but gentle, uncertain swirls of breeze are welcome and wonderful. J. very still and pensive but I think O.K.

On closer inspection maybe it is a crazy day. Puffs of breeze come up from every direction turning the bright hulls of the moored boats in random opposition. Harbor Patrol launch slowly creases the bay intent on some benign errand. Not much air for the two or three girls wind surfing. Altogether a slightly silly scatter of aquatic toys littering the diamond sparkle of sea. Print yourself, flash and dazzle, print this gull-embroidered horizon, this beckoning, chalky blue sfumato onto my brain. Print deeper than my rot, deeper than the scorch of all chemicals to come. I will need you, safe harbor, broad and spangling and opening into the greater sea.

The trick today will be to avoid, so far as possible,

being maudlin. Please please help me out of this "last" rut: last replenishing the kitchen window bird feeder, last morning perusal of the *Sandwich Sentinel* on the deck, last boiling of the battered Little House kettle. I wish it weren't all true—come, morbid Meg, say *possibly* true. If I *felt* good, if at first glimpse of clear morning sky I could feel that old tug of hope and desire behind my breastbone, I know my "condition" would seem worse. Last times would be such an outrage. Something else is at work in me now, a desire for a print, a record of what has been so namelessly significant, so dear—but b., for what? For whom? For you, perhaps. No, I will keep these Brian-longings at bay today. I think I am dredging him up, projecting him in order to hurt myself. Brian, vaporous son, will you ever imagine your mother's last waking day at Little House? Stop it.

J. and I have made a private plan to avoid Val and Frank when they return from their cruise. When one of us spies the Valmar far on the horizon we're going to high tail it down the Cape a ways, sit in some other anonymous sun for an hour or two and then, when the proverbial coast is clear, slip back into our empty digs. I will, I think, insure our non-meeting by leaving a cheery note saying we're not only dining out, but going to the movies. That should do it. I know V. & F. have to get back to Tarrytown tonight. J. can break the news later about Tests and Decisions. Then I will talk to Val on the telephone and open the floodgates. Funny, this need to buffer myself from a more public knowing. But necessary too—the last thing a hurt animal needs is the buzz of other animals' concern and distress. They can love me later.

Back from clandestine outing. A little midgie-ish on the dock, but we endure the periodic little pin-pricks anyway for the sake of the air and the lavender, oily light across the bay. Drank a glass of wine but can't remember taking a sip. Not a word exchanged on the subject, but there is an engulfing, irresistible sense of Last in each darkening moment.

J. reduces the Stop 'n Shop roaster to sheer skeleton. I do not freeze the bones for a future soup. There are in the larder a six-pack carton of tuna packed in water, most of a bottle of honey, many quart cans of chicken broth, a mostly full box of Tetley tea bags, sundry bottled spices. All will keep, I think. I leave them to their alien futures. We clear out the fridge, saving a little milk for morning tea, and a few slices of bread for toast. I will leave the books I brought on the shelves, even, I think, good old Alice Munro. Soul sister that you are, I can't imagine coming back to you. My summer duds, including toiletries, do not quite fill up a mid-sized Wells School duffle bag. Could this be possible? I've been here two months! What was going on those summers we loaded trunk, roof rack, and every conceivable millimeter of the station wagon's interior to journey a couple hundred miles to a fully furnished house on the Cape. How "low impact" I have grown.

Good for the environment. Environment seems to be nudging me along toward no impact. A lesson here.

Feeling a little woozy in the sitting room, and J. tells me to go to bed. Unpleasant taste in my mouth, temperature about 100. Too much feeling at headquarters.

I know I should sign off, b., turn off the light, but I think I am struggling in a kind of sick-sparrow way to keep the light on, just one light, a light in a little cottage on a little point by the sea. Let me be at least that much this night. No more unbearable lasts.

It's not that I am afraid of the dark. It's just that I do not quite care for the dark's company. This of course has not always been the case. Night used to be sweet release, launching me on all sorts of agreeable travels, conscious and un-. But to have been so bluntly shown those pictures of festering malignancies busily colonizing my interior, I feel somehow in the company of an unwanted Other. It's as if those blurry little -*nomas* are not only undoing me and transforming me into them, they are eavesdropping in the process, taking their smug measure of me. Again, fear plays no part in it. It's just that I don't want to sleep with those resourceful aliens making their gruesome plans. At least awake I can keep a beady inner eye out. Do they know their chemo is coming? This is not going to be like invading the Falklands, busters.

Oh, Meg, how you talk. You make yourself tired. Come, come to bed, J. Good night, beloved b. Out, lamp.

September 11

Back to Wells and School House. Drive not good. Felt shaky when we got in the car, then got worse. Sick-sour taste from my mouth all the way down. Very panicky. Tried lying down but made it worse. Tried separating enormity of feeling, especially as we got off the Cape and I could sense the sea receding behind us, from my miserable soma, but no good. Malaise embraces everything.

No lunch on the road—once a pleasure. Poor J. Made Wells by 3, and I went straight up to make up the bed and got in. Dozing and waking since. J. sweetly brought up tea on a tray (bad cup), sat with me.

House is feeling very sturdy in its stones, and I feel very far inside it, so weak in its midst. Not fit company, b. Sorry.

Up and down all night. Depositing, replenishing fluids. Took some aspirin—forgot about aspirin—and possibly in consequence slept and sweated a bit, woke up feeling a little restored. Fever down.

J. off early to school. He said he would look after the Boston hospital arrangements. Bless his heart for knowing how much I didn't want to do that today. I will know the folks at Mass. General soon enough.

School House still feeling vast, substantial, cavernous. We've lived here more than twenty years and still, after a week or two away, I forget the rooms. Very strange, big houses. This morning still in my wrapper I padded along the upstairs hallway peering in at the guest bedrooms. Like museum exhibits, they are rather perfect in a sad subtle New England way: austere, of course, old but not really antique spindled bed posts, the beds themselves high and hard. Faded, vaguely oriental patterns on the bulbous night-table lamps. A knocked about but newly upholstered wing chair in each room, a dark bureau filched from the dormitories, perhaps a milky ceramic basin and pitcher on top, suggesting, feebly, morning ablutions of the last century. Stacks of clean white (school) towels and face cloths in the bathrooms, heaps of blankets and sheets in the linen closet. Four of these chambers, not counting Brian's and ours. It seems we have about three guests a year these days, yet something vaguely human manages to animate the rooms as I pass by. I think it is in the carpets, the warm reds and oranges and indigo of the "Persian" rugs that seemed suitably venerable and threadbare when John and I fetched them out of garage sales during our starving schoolmaster days.

Even without a light on, the walls of the upstairs hallway are astringently white. The glass and gold-leaf frames of John's Cambridge college prints give off an impersonal glimmer. The effect this morning, I decide, is really not very nice. It is certainly not an esthetic statement or domestic greeting from John and Margaret Greeve. It says instead: these are established and traditional spaces; never mind that the tradition is finally unidentifiable and rather alien to the sensibilities of your hosts. In truth, when we first came to Wells I took some care to appoint these rooms—set out those vestigial basins, re-shaded those ancient lamps, hung those etchings of ruined abbeys spotted in Vermont flea markets. I thought at the time I had done a pretty good imitation of what head-master's-house guest quarters ought to look like. Even then we rarely had a guest. Bad of me not to have considered it from a guest's perspective—which could only have been: neat, clean, slightly of another era, not really comfortable. And (I hope only subliminally) *don't stay.* Terrible really. But the carpets do say something nice to me as I pass all those open doors.

Downstairs is better. But I am so small in this house! Have I always been? There is at least color here—and big good pictures. How pleased with themselves the New England fathers must have been to have marked off these spacious, high ceilinged rooms. The effect is really created by the light, by the high windows. Down here the carpets are rather good and the wing chairs are deep burgundy and forest green. There are pictures (all reproductions) you want to look at, a sexy pre-Raphaelite girl doleful at her escritoire, Ophelia about to submerge under lily pads. There are polished boxes on polished tables. There are so many gilt-framed photos of the Greeves in every conceivable attitude that a casual observer would get the impression that we were a family of thirteen. And as with the upstairs, this downstairs illusion bears some analysis. Whence all this seeming opulence, these alcoves of cushy chairs and sofas snuggled arm to arm, this dark, jeweled den, this sleek sweep of futuristic kitchen appliances? Of course the protocols and pride and periodic state occasions of Wells School require a degree of comfort and taste. But we might be a touch grand in that department. Why? For whom? This morning it's merely making me tired on behalf of the maintenance and housekeeping staffs. But I will admit also that the colors are picking me up. I love the Cape, and Little House is a treasure, but I realize there is no color there. We left out the color.

Liv Upjohn called to welcome me home. Very sweet, but in a minute and a half I was drenched in sweat and wobbly in my knees. Yes, I told her, the Cape was wonderful, but a bothersome bug . . . Liv said she understood. "Everyone here had the bug this summer." Anarchically, wickedly, I made a mental x-ray of everybody at Wells riddled with blurry little cancers. A three-minute conversation and I needed to lie down for an hour.

Dozed and was wakened by the unearthly hooting of Arnold Leiber downstairs. He was seeking permission to snoop around after electrical problems he feared may have resulted from a bad storm over the weekend. He said there had been "surges" in Wells village and people suffered the devastation of television and other appliances. I didn't tell Arnold that I was impressed that nature still had the ingenuity to do such things inside people's houses. So I followed old Arnold from room to room while we checked things, finding only flashing clocks and VCRs which he blessedly reset and put right. These simple operations undo me, convince me always that a new appliance displaying the right time must be purchased as soon as possible. J., pretending to know better, retrieves the owner's manual from his chaotic file, then in an attitude of great sadness crouches down uncomfortably and begins to try things. Arnold, though stranger every minute, is such a godsend.

J. home at five. We go tomorrow, no less, to Boston. Dr. K. will have fast posted my pictures and findings to a reputedly excellent oncologist, a Dr. Felice. Could this be felicitous? We decide to tell Val and Frank after tomorrow. We agree that the Wells story should be that I have had a "scare" and that I need to be tested and watched for a while. J. also asked me, so sweetly, if I thought I was still up to editing the *Wells Quarterly*. Somehow I had put that right out of my mind. But I don't see why not. That kind of focused tedium might be very good for me—the fact that it actually has to get done and come out. Work of this type could be a salvation. I noted ominously this a.m. that, feeling weak and ashy, I could not engage in the *N.Y. Times* crossword. It wasn't hard, but I could not finish.

Salad, broth, a little stir fry, wine with dinner. J. back to school for some desk work. Before bed we watch a video episode of *Jewel in the Crown*. Perfect, deep, total immersion. Maybe Paul Scott—and all those beautiful actors—are the cure. Somebody involved must know all there is to know about –nomas.

Too tired to read. Medicine tomorrow. God help me, b.

September 13

Reprieve! Today just talk and preparation. Dr. Felice an imposing presence. Not at all soulful, like Dr. K., which is at this point quite O.K., as Dr. K., once he got word of my "involvement," could not begin to hide his hopelessness. Dr. F. is another story altogether. Big man, massive bony brow, not quite Neanderthal. I'm told oncologists, like internal medicine people, are extra smart, because they have to do so much analysis. I want Dr. F. to be very, very smart.

His first words: How are you feeling right now? Then, I don't think I have to tell you that your condition is very serious. He didn't, but his way of laying it all out made everything firm and official. I felt almost reassured as he summarized my involvements. No longer am I a cruelly targeted anomaly, but a legitimate member of an earnest legion of multiply-involved somebody-or-other's sarcoma patients. Amazingly, he wanted to examine me further, as if my file wasn't impressive enough. Mostly probes and peeps, but they also took two more little boxlets of my blood, along with a few x-rays. Mass. General's not too bad, I think, the parts I saw rather shiny and speedy, although the whole place seems a little inhumanly big. Before we went home, J. and Dr. F. and I sat down in his office and discussed my treatment. Basically, three things will happen to me. Certain of my bad patches are going to be irradiated, but that will be later, after the chemotherapy. Tomorrow I go in for my first course. There are two groups of medicines, one to poison the cancer, the other to detoxify the poisons. This requires an overnight. Just as well, as I am rather in a surrendering mood. Nothing experimental here, we are assured, but "new and improved" in Dr. F's estimation.

One rotten bit of news, however. I had somehow got it in my head that the chemotherapy would take the form of pills or another sulfuric frappe. No such luck— injected right in the tender crook of my arm. Wish he hadn't told me. I can only think of those shots the vet gave sweet Chester when he had to be put down. Poor baby knew what was up, I think. Couldn't move his hind legs any more and I could feel his little hum against my chest as he sat on my lap. The vet had to give a first shot, so the final shot wouldn't "burn." Clearly worked. Chester just went quiet and was gone. He never stirred. It was very, very final. I wouldn't mind one of those first shots. Might even consider the second one day . . .

What to expect: *everyone responds differently*, Dr. F. begins, and I am at once unsettled. I can expect, however, nausea and some vomiting, dry mouth, dry throat, loss of appetite (appetite?), possibly diarrhea, then constipation, dizziness, general weakness. There was more, but I let it wash over me without penetrating. Somehow I already know. Toward the end of the session, seemingly out of a fog, I heard Dr. F. saying that some women like to go out and find a wig at the outset, since it's not much fun to think about and awkward to do when the chemo's underway. I guess that's considerate on his part. I try to imagine diverting our drive back to Wells to seek out a wig shop. How is it I've never in my life seen a wig shop? There are sometimes wigs on plaster heads at the hairdressers, but I have always thought they were a kind of totemic expression of the spirit of the place. I picture walking up and down aisle after aisle of wigs with J. Would this be playful? Funny? Ghastly? I laugh out loud, and Dr. F. is startled. I explain I just had a funny thought about wigs. Now I can't clear my head of loony images: looking intently into J.'s eyes as I try on the platinum blonde, the bouffant, dreadlocks. "It's just a concern some women have," Dr. F. says warily. We leave it that I will check in tomorrow a.m. for the first course. Imagine the entrée.

Driving back to Wells I feel lightheaded, bereft. Why wait a day? J. breaks the silence: "Should we get a wig?"

Meg is funny: "You're probably all right for now, John, but I think I'll wait to see if I look cute like a baby." I don't want to think about a wig. (So why do I keep conjuring up these crazy pictures??) And in a gruesome way I *do* want to see my bald head.

Back home and a nap, a good moist nap. Will there be sleep after chemo? A little chicken, salad, broth for dinner. Decide to save a glass of wine for before bed. I don't really have an appetite for it, but after tomorrow who knows what will be possible to pass over the tongue.

Sat myself down in the den after supper and called Val. She went literally wordless for a minute, then was wonderful. She wanted to know how I was feeling *that moment*, then: was I afraid? I told her both things and realized as I did that it was a terrific relief to let it out, more accurately a terrific relief to have a soul mate like Val. She offered to come up and I think meant it, but I don't know. It might be awful to have anyone around if I'm retching and spewing from the chemo. It might be nice to have her at the bedside for a while later, if I'm granted some kind of convalescent plateau.

Bless Val's heart. She called me back ten minutes after we hung up to recommend, of all things, an approach to cure. It's apparently the work of a husband and wife team called the Chelseas or Kelseys, both M.D.s, who, Val says, do a lot of "non-invasive" work with cancer patients, including ones, like me, with poorish report cards. I can't remember whether she said some of her Tarrytown friends were big boosters of the Kelseys/ Chelseas or had actually been treated by them. Val, at any rate, could not have been more fervent. It's all done by eating fruits and vegetables, making—actually training yourself to make—positive inner pictures of what your body should be doing, and having a positive, can-do attitude generally. I told Val it's probably too close to D-day here for a purely non-invasive alternative. But by all means send the books. Who knows? Val says there is a kind of Kelsey/Chelsea sanitarium—although I'm sure I heard the word "ashram"—up in Vancouver where they live. Val made it sound like Lourdes. Can I see myself as a peach-headed, positive-thinking new initiate to the compound in Vancouver? Will my chemo disqualify me? After weeks of what felt depressingly like no development, the most consequential developments have now loomed up and are sweeping me away, seemingly without a chance to deliberate. Val has no scientific or medical acumen whatsoever, but what she had to say, sweet intentions aside, sounds appealing, although perhaps not the idea of removing myself to Vancouver. I'm not too proud to be cancer-involved, but I really don't think I want to dwell among a cancerous sisterhood. This is no doubt small of me and proud. But good old Val. She's been on the money before. Aren't I the kind of soul who should be in dialogue, not chemical warfare, with her nemesis?

Why is that approach never even a dimension of the medical response? Maybe it is now. Maybe the Kelseys/ Chelseas are the dawn of soulful healing. A little mental note is flickering: find Mary Baker Eddy's big book, figure out if Christian Science wasn't right all along. I hope I've got enough brain cells after this treatment to follow through. This evening it seems perfectly reasonable to think Mary Baker Eddy knew as much or more than beefy Doctor Felice. Meg, you old wing nut. Tomorrow you flush yourself out with violent chemicals, then if you get sufficient strength back, you plan to read books and watch videos explaining why you did precisely the wrong thing. Still, it's nice to think of Val speed mailing me promises of hope and cure.

Nice glass of wine with J. in the den. Suddenly very sleepy, almost giddy about the morning's trials. Night, b., Don't let me be a baby about the injection. Dream of wigs.

September 15

No good, b. Wretched, hateful chemo, wretched night, wretched day. Home now, feeling alone, small, pitiful, abandoned by science and medicine. Everything wrong, my poor ravaged body is outraged. A white roar inside my head. Sour, chalky feeling in my mouth all the way down. Stomach seizing up in sickening, sometimes unendurable cramps. No let up, nothing helps.

So this is what medicine thinks of cancer. If I were the cancer and survived this chemical assault, I would seek deadly revenge. This isn't me. This is the way technology, or maybe just men, go after illness. They want to scorch it, rip it out, beat the hell out of it. And I was all compliance. Please stop this, end this, end this.

September 16

Still cramping. I tried to remember how I felt before, couldn't. Nothing but water stays down, not even broth. Eating unthinkable. Glance at my face in the bathroom mirror—bright red. Please pass. Can't write, b.

September 17

Cramps are either easing, or I'm used to them. Sat down to pee this a.m., and nothing came, just a searing heat. I've apparently dried up. Water. I drink and drink, but it goes down like cotton. Now it won't come out. Where does it go? J. will call Dr. F. in Boston.

J. very upset. Said he can't get a helpful response from Dr. F. or anybody else there. I tell him I'm not right, and in that instant we both realize we don't know what to do. I tell J. I think I belong in the hospital, and then I'm too tired to talk, to help make the arrangements. This is terrible, b. I can see that John is beleaguered with Wells' snarls, has been all week. Hate drawing him into this hold. Let me disappear.

September 18

Cramps now just a steady ache, like heartburn. Dry and sour all through, can't eat, can't go. Out the window brilliant blue, leaves beginning to turn. No relation to me.

J. is taking me back to Mass. General to stay for a while. He has lined up another specialist, a Dr. Dietrich, to have a look. Highly recommended, J. says. Val's book and video await me on the night stand. Fruits and vegetables, happy thoughts, imagining my sarcoma breaking into bits and benignly washing away—road not taken.

Worried about J. Wells is no fun right now. Brian and I are raising, I know, unspeakable possibilities. There *is* Malevolence at work in the world, b. We are nothing before it. God help me.

September 19

All tucked in and wired up to my bed and related apparatus. To Mass. General this a.m. A cell to myself, which is pretty cushy, as the world reckons. I'm on I.V. now, my new best friend, and there is fluid once again in this sere carcass. So much better. My head is clear again. Bodily complaints seem laughably endurable. I feel oddly safe.

J.'s at the Copley Plaza! Strange to think of him moving up and down its plush corridors.

In a day or so, I'll be scanned again, and Dr. F. and this Dr. Dietrich can see if my *-nomas* survived the chemo any better than I did.

So strange, I've been an officially pitiful invalid for only a week or so, but my perceptions of the Healthy World are already altered forever. Now anybody actually walking about and purposeful seems enviably powerful. Doctors, nurses, aids are godlike in the ease with which they move through the room, the hospital, the now unimaginable world beyond. Why, I wonder, do I so quickly attribute a moral superiority to the physically able? It's actually obvious: the physically well are able to act, to contribute, to help make the world work. Invalids are, regarded without sentiment, a drain on community resources and energy. Even in tip-top shape, I might have been a bit of a drain on the community. If I recover, I'll atone.

So tired now, b. Maybe I can sleep a bit without fouling my wires.

September 20

Positively zooming through the Kelseys' *Seeing Clear of Cancer*. I love the way it doesn't even connect to medicine as actually practiced. Wonderful stories of people showing up with grapefruit-sized tumors in their bowels, holes the size of quarters in their bones, then all of it shrinking, dissolving, filling back in. Very sweetly biblical. Something in me wants to call the Kelseys, get the numbers of the cured, have them tell me in reasoned cadences that, yes, they've never felt better. I don't of course; mainly I suppose because I don't want to find out otherwise. But why not, really? If the body somehow created a culture for cancers to fester, surely it could create one where cancer was unwelcome. Until I had it, my body seemed to know how to keep cancer at bay. And in me the Kelseys would certainly have an instructive negative case study. Who in history has spent more of her waking hours immersed in negativity, dark analysis, and doubt? Who has more willfully passed by vegetables greening on their stalks, berries dew-glistening in morning sun, melons in bounteous heaps at the Stop 'n Shop, while whole schools of unlucky tuna have been hauled untimely from the sea, column after column of depressed, shackled, indoor chickens have lost their foreshortened lives on my account. And, finally, how beautiful to sit in a sun dappled garden or, in winter, a graceful lounge overlooking the majesty of Canadian Rockies while casting a steady inner eye on the amoebic particles of your immune system as, full of resolve, they encircle the cancerous intruder, disarm, detoxify, and gently dissolve him. Oh, I would like to meditate such a treatment even without an assurance of cure. Such a sweet way to treat sister body. Bless you, Val. Bless you, Kelseys, I'd vote for you both for President.

September 21

Liberated from Mass General this a.m. It felt so good to be disconnected to my tubes, to get free of that lobster-like bed, all of the adjustments to which bend me in ways I don't want to bend. Wrong, wrong—all of it, the charts, the checks, the jabs, the probes, the outrageous suggestions to pee at odd hours, the meaningless food. Only one more Course, God help me. The whole business makes me feel unworthy of the Kelseys.

J. planned a sweet thing on the way home—but it turned sad. Not his fault. It was such a deliciously bright blue alpine day, J. suggested we detour our trip back to Wells and call in at Little House. He wanted to settle a few things with Jenkins about shutting off water and hauling the Valmar anyway. At first it seemed nice to shed Boston like fussy, busy, trafficky skin, but I forgot how forlorn the Cape can feel after Labor Day, the car-less drive-in theaters by the dazzling light of midday, the desolate Dairy Queens and lobster roll joints. The shimmer and sparkle of sky and water as we drove high over the Cape Cod Canal was diamond bright—but nothing like summer. Even the gusts swishing past the windshield seemed to say "later," "over," "gone."

I wish I'd never reentered Little House. Dark and still, just—of course—as we left it, so vacated that its emptiness was an insistent presence. I couldn't bear the familiar must in the air, the aggravated hum of the refrigerator. Jenkins was nowhere to be found. From a great label-less jug we left on top of the fridge, J. poured us two glasses of not-quite-gone-to-acid white zinfandel which we drank on the blowy deck looking out over the choppy, almost empty harbor, rigging clanking somewhere, gulls. It was not restful. Felt as though we were waiting someplace unfamiliar in the wind. J. locked up and said, for some reason, "Good-bye, Little House."

Very melancholy driving off the Cape toward Wells. Neither of us said much, nor did music seem right on the tape machine. As we cleared New Bedford and headed toward Providence, it occurred to me with remarkable clarity how really poor these little not-quite-seaside towns are. Shoreham nearly broke my heart, the whole main drag a sequence of storefronts unimaginable to enter. Impromptu hair salons, nail care, used children's clothes, a closed-down carpet and tile store, closed-down bed and bath shop, more hair and nail care, closed pizzeria, uneatable Chinese take-out place, auto parts, for rent, for rent, for rent. The only life a tumble of patrons and matrons moving in and out of 24 Hour Deli. On the roof is a listing white plywood sign with black-painted letters: XEROXING, FAX. Poor Shoreham. No more fishing, no more canning, no more mill work inland. No one wants a summer place in Shoreham. No one wants to put in a boat at the oily, littered, faintly foul town slip. Nothing to do in Shoreham. The squeamish Cape papers report cocaine has come to Shoreham. Who buys it? What are the rituals of its use? How are the tee-shirted, tattooed young men of Shoreham transformed by cocaine? We buy a paper and J. uses the men's at 24 Hour Deli/XEROXING, FAX.

Behind a tired shelf or two of long-unwatched action videos of the past decade, I spot the luridly colorful cartons enclosing the pornography selections. Unlike anything else in Shoreham on this blanching September afternoon, these come-ons are pulsing, livid, sure of themselves. We drive out of Shoreham, and I form the dismal equation: Shoreham is to town as my condition is to me. I want so much to cry.

Once again, Head's House when we arrive at Wells seems monumental, cavernous, also where I belong. J. brings me broth, chicken snips, and salad in bed. Read, got lost in Edna SVM's poems, confide grimly in b. and, spent, surrender. Bless J. for his hopes for this day. Bless you, too.

September 23

Another lazy day. Night sleep has been so strangely light. I become a hummingbird just below the surface of consciousness, to which I arise every few hours. I crave something deep and dark, the full descent, not this anxious hovering.

This a.m. I silently beheld my J. as he rose, showered, dressed and otherwise girded himself for the world. Poor baby, he tells me only a little and with wise good humor, but I know when school is hurting him. There is a flash of—yes—outrage in his eyes, a set of the mouth, a rigidity between collar and belt. The "issues" don't seem to matter any more; that is, they certainly don't matter to me. J., who has seen surely every variety of bad schoolboy behavior, cannot be knocked off center by what happens, but he is still too mortally vulnerable to everybody's meanness. Can't rest, literally, if one or another of his privately unhappy colleagues projects bad will or deviousness onto him or a decision he has made, invariably with great patience. Why aren't my prayers for him answered? Why hasn't he come to know, now and forever, that he is all right, sound, valued, loved, imperfect but very, very fine? How come any spotty fifteen-year-old who has pinched an illicit hookah from a spotty friend's closet can call up such depthless disappointment and worry in my J.? How can boys who behave like thugs in the course of football games—as if football itself were not an invitation to assault and battery—unsettle J. at fifty-six to the point he cannot take up a forkful of food? And when the heads of schools and coaches of teams who play foul decide not to notice, why does this surprise J.? He is not inclined to nostalgia; he does not claim to have seen a better day. Is this perhaps his best quality, this inability not to feel precisely as bad as others want him to feel? Folly, malevolence, ignorant surmises hurt him. What dark, sad, prior-life part of him lets him absorb, store up the sins of the world as his own? Is this why I love him so? Is this why I, so deceptively and brainily unflappable, hate, I mean *hate* the self-absorbed and mean-spirited colleagues who bring him down, the effete weasels who let Wells School feed them three hot meals a day, furnish, heat, clean, and improve charming flats and houses for them, pay them a livable salary to teach 150 minutes a day for eight and a half months a year? I have learned—but why hasn't J.— that awful people are shrewdly good at awfulness. They are not clumsy or superficial in their slights and affronts.

They know, for instance, that they don't even have to question J.'s integrity and ability to devastate him; they need only to perform badly themselves. John will suffer on their account. He will take himself to task and let others take him to task for anything wrong, mean or shabby at school. As if his capacity for hurt were infinite. And is this how Wells thrives? By allowing every awful person to escape the deadening burden of his and her awfulness by letting J. take it on. For he will. He always will. And aren't I a big help? A dried up, sour-mouthed bag of bones, toxic fluids pulsing fitfully through her vessels in search of still more toxic intruders. After bad days and dark hours, J. will look at me and say, "So Wells comes to this?" Poor sweet baby will never say, but he doesn't have to say, so wife comes to this? So just what is his capacity for deadly empathy? I hope it is vaster than I can fathom, but it cannot be infinite. God help us.

Stop. This day did not begin in such gloom. It began with a vision of J. standing at his bureau. He had just stepped into his shorts, his hair still wet and tousled from the shower. His hands were placed lightly on the bureau top, creating an impression that he might be posing some grave silent question to the mirror. I believe he was just resting, one of those morning pauses before the will sets one in terrible motion.

Very nice to take a long anonymous measure of the man I have loved so much. Morning sun somehow irradiated the drawn shades to create a pearly grey light in the room, perfect atmosphere for not-yet-day. Such a man, standing so still beyond the foot of the bed. Still a very beautiful man. I'm so lucky to have a tall, rangy J., that great vulnerable stretch of back, the good nubs of his spine, the sharp symmetry of shoulder blades. For the longest time he didn't move. What must he have been thinking? Was it thought? I hope it was pure feeling. Oh, b., the beautiful back, the beloved milky skin. J., I thought, you are so exposed. Behind that precious wonderful back, the worst could happen, no doubt will.

I remember that back burnt brown, color of coffee and cream, glistening with cold salt water. J. had gotten Geoff Dusenberry's old yawl for the honeymoon, and it somehow seemed due to us that there would be a week of unbroken July sunshine, light but steady air, and plenty of room to put in at every cove. I can see us, feel us at anchor off Cuttyhunk. Five o'clock and the late sun still a pleasantly needling presence on face and neck, back and sides. It occurred to J., most modest of men, that we should be naked every possible second. Or was that empathy, too? If so, bless him, bless that insistent sun, the caressing puffs, the creaking, rocking hull of that sweet old boat. Below decks, nuzzling in the cockpit, standing brazenly at the bow, thigh to thigh, cock to belly, nipple to rib, J.'s great warm brown hand clasping the back of my neck. That week, b., there was no beginning or end to it.

No one had to tell us a thing. We would row the dinghy to shore, cadge some yacht club shower and emerge to find each other irresistible to the touch. Any dockside bar was hilarious. Nobody ever knew as much as we did. But at Pocasset we didn't know enough to get out of the rain when, eating our lobster under what we thought were the stars, it started to rain like stink and we were soaked to the skin before we could rise from the table. We were insane, but also inspired, to board our dinghy in the deluge. As it filled up to the point of swamping, we paddled around hysterically from mooring to mooring, looking without aid of flashlight for our yawl. Of course we found it. We were in the great grip. We were in thrall. There is no getting dry from salt water, but we made dry, silky skin. There is no getting warm, even in summer, on a stormy night on the water, but we were snug as babies. I remember a buttery kerosene lantern hanging over the sink below, all night ripples of dull gold washing back and forth over our gold-rosy skin as the boat rose and fell, rocked and creaked. Oh, that was sex, b. How beautiful to fall into that oceanic knowing while moving with the ocean itself. It did not start or stop, there was only the holding fast, rocking together, the greedy blindness, the swimming over and into each other; saying yes to it all, yes to everything. So powerfully blessed to have learned then that the depth of sex is not in any act—I forget our acts—but in the realization that in all of it we were, I was, held fast in the larger dance. J. and I were there, then, tuned to that surely cosmic, surely eternal frequency. *That*, readers of manuals, swallowers of hopper-uppers, is the truth. That is the point. Did we come together? Beside the point. We were rapt together, held fast in the bigger thing. He came, I came, came and came. Only in the misty morning, by no means first light, did I awake in my salt water-chafed and rather chilly flesh, lying atop bed clothes seemingly as damp as I was. At the foot of our berth, J.'s white little-boy's bum and long brown back. Making coffee for us. There could be no plan for such a morning. The three or four days ahead of us were incalculably vast, brighter than the spangling horizon. In a minute there would be hot coffee and all of J.'s long brown delicious self. "Meg," he said. "Do you know how much I love Pocassett?"

Broth, salad, one of those paper thin ribbons of steak. Not disagreeable. I will be strong like bull. J. at a meeting till late; maybe a glass of wine with him then. It's been a nice, nice day with you, b. Maybe there is life after chemo.

September 24

In and out of shallow sleep again. Awoke this a.m. still so full of J. Maybe it's being laid waste and useless, but I have been feeling so utterly open to him. At the exact moment in my life where I can do nothing whatsoever for him, I want to do anything for him. I wish, like Prospero, I could bewitch his school into perpetual serenity. With his old bird beak lying here stewing in her prescribed poisons while his willowy prodigal son is M.I.A. somewhere across the Atlantic, the very least Wells School could do would be to behave itself civilly for a term or two.

Last night before lights out J. was feeling burdened by the obligation to undertake a new Long Range Plan for Wells. I could swear Wells and maybe every school in the world wants to make a new Long Range Plan every ten minutes. Long Range Plan. What a majestic sounding load of rubbish. Where did the rhetoric come from? Lenin and Stalin? The brave and sweeping Five Year and

Ten Year Plans can hardly have been an inspiration. If my recall of Modern Russian history 201 and 202 is reliable, none of those Soviet plans came to anything, causing the plan rhetoric to change. "Planning," "Long Range," "Strategic," "goals," "mission"—the lingo has a sort of wearying go-ahead jingoism to it, a certain kind of materialist's hedge against despair. What can the slings and arrows of outrageous fortune do in the face of a mighty Long Range Plan? More cruelly to the point, what can a private school's ponderous Long Range Plan do in the face of a ravenous, utterly unplanned commercial culture? Against the caprices of geothermal or ecological surprises? Against the concentrated ill will of a single hateful soul? Not a gawd-damn thing, as Jenkins would say.

How stupid and insensitive—redundant terms, mutually equivalent—can Truax and his board chums be to ask J. of all people to make a Long Range Plan now. The man's son is apparently A.W.O.L., and his wife seems to be passing from coal to ash, and you ask him to set about thinking very concretely about the Long Range. So nice of you, Bill Truax. And pardon me, Admiral Scott, I know you're very cold, but what exactly are your plans for your next expedition? Don't, don't, don't you dare make a Long Range anything, J. Instead I want you to look back or underneath or wherever and locate a shimmering auroral moment, some pulsing Pocasset, of your deep heart. Find that instant, hold it fast, enter it as you would a bubble and let it expand, ascend, come rosily to life. That's long range planning. That and only that.

Lunch of chicken noodle soup and buttered toast, almost nice. Some chocolate milk, less nice. I've got to fatten up. Two nights ago I was less than a hundred, my seventh grade weight. Called the Alumni Office and breezily asked them to give J. the *Quarterly* proofs to take home for my red pencil. Meg is breezy: medicines are bothersome but I'm back on my feed/feet again, and, yes, I heard the last-minute math replacement can't keep her fourth-formers in the room, and yes, I've heard that all the coaches are furious at Arnold for not lining the fields, that the state-funded peanut butter is gagging the boys, that Constance Benoit has walked out on Philip and has taken a garage apartment in Wells village, that . . . And here I tell a lie, b. I say someone is at the door and I have to go. Nobody, thank God, is at the door. I sit perfectly still for fifteen minutes. There is a thin sheen of perspiration all over my body. My husband is Headmaster, and I am utterly nauseated by school.

Then some nice and perhaps important personal archival work. Moved by God knows what, I start nosing through my very first b.'s from Radcliffe, see that I include what are either lecture notes or maybe reflections on them. I could feel again how heady it all was, the daily grind so thin and insubstantial compared to the force and color of ideas. I see in the spring of my twentieth year I took pains to copy out a dark and rather terrifying passage from Nietzsche:

> There is an ancient story that King Midas hunted in the forest a long time for the wise Silenus, the companion of Dionysus, without capturing him. When Silenus at last fell into his hands, the King asked what was the best and most desirable of all things for man. Fixed and immovable, the demigod said not a word, till at last, urged by the king, he gave a shrill laugh and broke out into these words: "Oh, wretched ephemeral race, children of chance and misery, why do you compel me to tell you what it would be most expedient of you not to hear? What is best of all is utterly beyond your reach: not to be born, to be *nothing*. But the second best for you is—to die soon.

After which, Meg Chasin, modest Radcliffe sophomore, writes: "When I understand this, I will understand everything." I cannot remember reading the passage, copying it out, wishing to understand it, although I do seem to recall wanting to understand everything. Egomaniacal girl—what a wish!

Which led me to wondering when and why I read Nietzsche—I can only remember Zarathustra careering down his mountainside. A bit of sleuthing in the by no means reliable Greeve document files, and I see from my spring semester sophomore report card that I was indeed enrolled in a course titled German Romantics (got an A). But is Nietzsche anything like a Romantic? Wouldn't he be awfully late? I dimly remember reading Goethe. Could the course have spanned Goethe to Nietzsche, possibly to show what happened to German romanticism? Or did I get inspired to read Nietzsche on my own? Something Philip Lowenthal said or read could have driven me to N. Was I being merely grandiose or was I more on the edge than I want to remember to have written: "understand this, and I will understand everything." This to an oracle claiming it is best never to be born, next best to die soon. I am certain I harbored no wish not to have been born, nor, really ever, a desire to die. But if I read myself literally, my twenty-year-old desire was just to understand this sentiment, not to possess it. For a vital person, one rather full of herself at that, to come to terms with not being was and is a tall order. What on earth was I thinking?

Buried myself for an hour in the chaos of the Greeve non-library looking for Nietzsche. Find at last Walter Kaufman's Modern Library ed. of *Basic Writings*—J.'s. Gratifyingly I find by dumb luck the passage in question toward the beginning of the *Birth of Tragedy*, and lo, it's not Nietzsche at all, but N. quoting Sophocles in *Oedipus at Colonus*. So it's a much more ancient "everything" I was hoping to understand at twenty.

Now I can't get the damned passage out of my head. Gruesome thing. "The second best for you is—to die soon." Thanks very much. I'm quite well enough on my way as it is. And for the record, I would prefer Pocasset, or even the appetite for a good meal. But that passage; it keeps snuggling up to me. It makes a tug, it wants to hurt me, make me cry. Get lost, Nietzsche or Sophocles. Away from me, specter, crow. And shame on you, Deep Meg, for seeking out that passage—scripted carefully into your pages from the outset, b.

J. home late again tonight, but I'll wait to eat with him. Funny and very sweet that he's the only company I want.

Need to clear my head. Think I'll shampoo and shower, which will literally clear my head. Poor head. I'm looking a bit like the elderly Ben Franklin or, in a more somber mood, like a de-wigged *ancien regime* aristocrat being carted from prison cell to guillotine, as rendered in the etchings in the "good" guest room. Poor J. I'll put on one of my perky kerchief get-ups for dinner. At last, a thought to lighten my heart: the wig. Oh, if I only had one, anything. I'd like J. to open the door to behold a weirdly bespectacled Dolly Parton or a flashing-eyed (through weird spectacles) raven-haired Ava Gardner. No, I wouldn't, I wouldn't at all.

But I will shower, shampoo what tufts of hair choose to hang in there. Then something else mindless, the over preparation of a modest supper, who knows, television. Love you, b.

September 25

Decision to make. Drs. Felice and Dietrich told John it would be O.K. to delay course two of the chemo for a few days in light of my being so ravaged by the first dose. Appealing, but I wonder about the ultimate value of gaining a mouse-increment of strength before the next siege. Better maybe to get the hell of it over with. Truth is, I don't want it at all, ever again. What's wrong with me, anyway? Chasins were never robust stock, I suppose, but it was always hearts. How did I get to be the cancer type? Why couldn't I at least have been a Kelsey type? I might have been gliding seraphically around bright gardens in Vancouver, mentally picturing health. How is it that sitting here in the grey gloom of this kitchen over a rather bitter cup of tea (out of milk, again), feeling stuffed with stale straw from adam's apple to toe, I can still be smugly dismissive of imagined Kelsey initiates with their mantras of lovely thought? I don't feel superior to them so much as annoyed by their willingness, for their aging bodies' sake, to be sweet and simple. That's exactly what's wrong with me—a refusal, or constitutional inability to be sweet and simple. I may have just answered my own question about why I'm the cancer type.

Here's another puzzle I'd like to figure out, b. And I have a powerful premonition I'm going to figure it out whether I like it or not. How come, since I can't even remember when—last March? Possibly even last fall—I felt normal or "well," I still know (even though I can't feel) what normal and well are? I feel bad, chalkily, ashenly bad, and I also know it's bad; it's like a droning in the tissues, almost a current, telling me *wrong, wrong, wrong, wrong.* So in Deep Meg headquarters something *knows* this whole cancer malaise-feeling is wrong, but in order to know it, it—the knower—can't itself be wrong or sick. So something deep in the core of me is neither sick nor wrong. Here's the puzzle: what is the relation-ship of my not-sick knower to the sickness? Why is the sickness prevailing over the knower in my sour, shrinking body? Will the knower always know, always be well? And if so, won't I hurt and suffer titanically when the body gives up and fails finally? Because the knower will register that, too. I have a feeling what the Kelsey cult wants to do is to pacify and charm the knower into taking healthy charge of the body again. The method is to be sweet and simple and thus give the knower a kind of prayerful per-mission to step up to the task. I'm pretty sure this is

Mary Baker Eddy's terrain as well, although her approach was more daring, *literally* out of this world. She decided that the knower was the only self and thus always and forever well. Whereas Socrates said, I always felt sensibly, that we have a divine and thus immortal spark or germ in our mortal souls, MBE says that's the whole soul, whole self. The rest, and I have always loved this, *isn't even there.* My cancer, my jumpy, tingly skin, my rasping pipes are all an illusion. Meditation, faith, and prayer will help me to see this. But when they don't, and they don't, the illusion is awfully hard to put aside, especially when you are sicking up pure bile and passing black blood into the plumbing.

Again, it's the relationship, the real relationship, between the whole and well knower and the sick known I want to understand. Does my knower stand in relation to my cancerous system as God stood in relation to Job? He was there all right, but he wasn't, until that suspect epilogue, eager to interfere with what was going on. I shouldn't speak for animals, but I am certain that when poor old Chester met his maker at the vet's, he was just plain sick. He experienced it all, every grating pain, but he didn't also know he was sick and what an awful insult that was to the true Golden Labrador condition. How do you know, the Sophist pipes up. Chester too may have gone into that good night in profound doggy bitterness and despair. But he didn't. He just didn't, and I know it. I was there. He was on my lap. Chester exhaled the breath of life right over the back of my hand. He was sick, but he was untroubled by any knower. I could see it in the beautiful golden pools of his eyes. Even those last days when he could not raise his hind legs off his smelly mat, he wriggled himself in reflexive joy when he heard me rattling the Biscuits bag. Oh, and in the morning when I'd come downstairs—he was as generously happy to see me as when we first brought him home. But he couldn't get up. His eyes beamed and then they ached at me, not because he was failing and he knew it, but because he couldn't get up.

Old Meg does not mind eating meals in which wood chips and ashes pass over sandpaper down into cramped and roiling depths. She doesn't mind hummingbird sleep. She doesn't mind the (actually fascinating) image of a startled, balding owl in the morning mirror. She minds that she is failing, diverted from keen sensation, wonder, and love by something purposeful and rotten. She is even failing ahead of schedule for females of her culture. She minds because she knows. She knows better.

A bad, no maybe a good, cry. I don't know. Why bother thinking—you only fall apart. I suppose it's the specter of Course Two and having to make a decision. Oh, come home, J. Come home armored from niggling, needy, greedy Wells. Come home to greedy, needy Meg. She'll rig up her most tantalizing kerchief. There will be candles flickering over the tuna and celery. Anyway, there will be a drink and a fire and at least one good thing. Come home, J. Come home, come home, come home.

September 26

Shame on me for the muling and puling. The point, B., is to be a vivid witness to what happens, not to fog up the lens with whining and self-pity. Strength, book-y.

After a terrible, fluttery sleep, good talk with J. about Course Two. No appreciable strength is going to be gained in an extra two or three days. Having the dreadful prospect on the horizon makes for a kind of illness in itself, so full steam ahead to Mass. General on Monday morning. God help me. It is certainly easy to imagine the chemo shriveling and desiccating my cancers, but I can't picture (*pace*, Kelseys) the rest of me withstanding the siege. I am ninety-eight pounds this a.m. I have a head like William Frawley's in "I Love Lucy." I have the pallor of oysters in milk. Yet, with what I am sure must be deep inner reserves of pith and pluck, I will take on Course Two.

J. may stay over a night at the Copley Plaza, but he has to be back at Wells for some messes and state occasions. How nice just to go unconscious and miss the purge altogether.

Started to have bad thoughts, which turned into good thoughts, about Brian. Just as I was about to begin lashing myself again with worries for his safety and well-being, with sheer missing, there was a curious reprieve. So clear: I *don't want* Brian to know how I am, to see me like this—certainly not yet. If there's recovery of any kind or length after Course Two, I want to achieve it before I see my baby. J. tells me only a little because he doesn't want to upset me, but I know he's been frantic to get in touch with Brian, even to the point of rustling up unfortunate acquaintances of Brian's youth. One thing is fairly certain: save a miracle, I will not see Brian before tomorrow, so all the more reason to get on with the rest of the chemo. Logically, if I'm going to see Brian again, it's going to be after. So presto! Seeing my son becomes an incentive to get the treatment out of the way. Brian, you sweet, goofy, impossible boy, I will drink twelve gallons of spring water a day, half that again of carrot juice, eat plate after mounded plate of sliced zucchini, beet greens, chick peas, and arugula, grow back at least a pixie length of hair for you. Your feeble and selfish mother has so little innate vitality that she'd, most days, sell her ticket to Course Two for three full days of ordinary, pre-cancerous vigor. But for you, willowy shadow-son, she will bravely scorch and scald, cramp and retch. For you, beloved, maddening boy, anything.

Today I was a ghost all afternoon. Football and soccer weekend at school, unearthly bright day, air positively charged. J. sneaked home for a quick sandwich with me on the back terrace, then back to the matches. Even inside the house I could hear the ebb and flow of football, the faint rising and falling of cheers, insistent but indistinct syllables from the stadium p.a., the hollow booming of a drum. All that clashing, bashing and tearing about, and I a molting sparrow, elegantly caged, attentive and alone. The bright leaves and sky through the mullions, the muffled football cadences felt strangely reassuring. All's right with the world. Maybe this is how I have always wanted it, the dramas of the bright noisy world going on as expected, at a safe distance from me. Sitting at the kitchen table, scratching out little infelicities in the sentences of the contributors to the *Wells Quarterly*, I am, I suppose, auditing the world outside this house, just as I am auditing the games. I rather like it that way. Moreover, I fancy that, despite its relentless optimism, the autumn number of the *Wells Quarterly* will read well. Peck, peck, scratch, scratch. There, to one side, in that bush, a sparrow makes a contribution.

J. had to dine with faculty and families of the athletes, so I, on the brink of inserting the *Churchill Between the Wars* video, spied the *Brideshead* set, and started that instead. So glad. Silly, rarefied, beautiful boys in their own impossible world—funny story to watch on the margin of

Wells School. Charles and Sebastian were getting drunk on the Flytes' vintage wines when I fell asleep. Brian is somehow with the *Brideshead* boys. J. taps me on the shoulder, fuzz on the screen. I sit up and say, "Off to chemo," not a brain cell working. No. J. says, and holds me. Monday.

Sweet J. brings me soup, buttered toast, some cut up fruit. No food allowed after noon tomorrow, not that I ever want anything. But I refuse to give cancer the satisfaction of shriveling me past recognition. Ninety-eight pounds! Although my face looks all right, in my opinion.

Sunday tomorrow. Light duties for J. After church Brahms on the stereo? Nice, feel very loving of Brian today. And J., always.

September 27

Bad day all day, because of church.

Drove into St. Stephen's in Cos Cob for, we believed, the choir, but we only got the children's choir. Dispirited and oddly harsh little voices, the wayward, contra-musical sound that can only be produced by children singing against their will.

But that was not the problem. The problem was probably me and the poisonous attitude I no doubt carry with me everywhere. B., I felt myself sitting in that pew just like a cranky and ill old woman. Who *was* that agitated little sourpuss in the peculiar kerchief? My hopes for the service were probably unrealistic. I wanted worshipful quiet. In that worshipful quiet I wanted to pray. I wanted to pray for grace and strength as I undergo Course Two. But it was impossible. I'm not sure why it surprises me that you get no rest in an Episcopal service. Somewhere early on the Anglican fathers thought it was a good idea to keep folks standing up and sitting down. Perhaps they believed this kept everyone alert. Between the standing up and sitting down, there is very little time to juggle the service leaflet, *Book of Common Prayer*, and the hymnal. Am I the only Episcopalian who feels the need of a desk and a secretary to negotiate the liturgy?

Everything made me mad. Even J. gave me a funny look when I declaimed, probably too loudly, "all things visible and invisible" over the new mistranslation "all things seen and unseen" in the Nicene Creed. It's not a small point. My Lord of the universe created things mortals can never see, strictly *invisible* things; the *unseen* includes things people just don't happen to notice. What problem to modern understanding did the words "visible" and "invisible" pose? I suppose continuously altering sacred, familiar texts is part of the same approach to worship that likes to have you standing up and sitting down all the time. I know what I need. I need to find a quiet, ill-attended Catholic church, preferably in the middle of the week when there is no hint of a service. I just want to sit there in the close and holy dark, maybe light a candle for my beloved, and pray until my heart breaks. May the Catholics forgive me. God knows.

The sermon was disgraceful. It was a reflection on what it means to "fear" God, when God is love. Not an unpromising puzzle, but in the logic and language of the young associate rector, who, J. told me, runs the parish's youth program although the youth don't like him, it all turned to mush. He did give one good example, though. He talked about how he was really afraid to come unprepared or to submit superficial work to an esteemed professor at his college. This kind of fear, it was suggested, was compatible with a loving, if demanding, deity. But then the associate rector badly lost his way. He had read some little self-help book—or perhaps several of them— and had pounced on the bromide that it is possible—and more often right than we might think—to love seemingly opposite or mutually antagonistic things. This, he said more than once, smiling like a jack-o-lantern for emphasis, was "both/and" loving, which has a lot to commend it over "either/or" loving, which he believed was now culturally narrow and outdated. Both/and: Belfast Protestants and IRA, Bosnians and Serbs, Palestinian Arabs and Zionists. It didn't help that I was also feeling very queer—a line of sharp discomfort, like heartburn moving in waves between my breastbone and belly. Suddenly I was soaked in perspiration and was about to ask J. to leave, when it abated a little. Could have been divine retribution for uncharitable thoughts.

The offering was welcome because we got to sit still, and Communion was fine, except for the fussy qualifications in the eucharistic prayer,

Most humbly beseeching thee to grant
that, by the merits and death of thy Son Jesus

Christ, and through faith in his blood, we and
all thy whole church, may obtain remission of
our sins, and all other benefits of his passion.

Which must have been composed by lawyers. I took
the sacrament and prayed for grace, for Brian and for J.

Drive back to Wells was lovely—was, well, autumnal.
Bright, clear sky. Leaves from banana-yellow to scarlet,
but also plenty of green in our valley. Back home, still a
little queasy in my mid-section. Starvation? Fear of
Course Two? Probably. Also cancer. Too preoccupied and
uncomfortable to enjoy the Brahms. Sherry didn't feel
good going down.

Miserable, self-obsessed, worthless woman. So sorry,
b. Help me. God help me. The way out is through, or so
I've always told others. *Learn* from this. No matter what
it is, learn.

To Boston at six a.m. Poor J.

October 1

Back to Wells, but not quite back to life.

Worse than I thought. Hell is never depicted in terms of taste. Sulfur, salt, vomit—like a dry powder in my mouth, down the throat. Everything, every sip of water carries it. I can taste it in my skin. I have only been to Boston, but I have tasted hell.

Can't shake the episode of Tuesday night. The cyclical cramping seemed to come to something ultimate, horrible, final. Like the last contraction of childbirth; a monstrous aping of childbirth. I could no longer control or moderate it at all. I had evacuated everything, but still the sickening pressure to pass a hopeless weight. Felt like, maybe was, my body's frenzied attempt to be clean. I believed it would happen in an unthinkable hemorrhage. That, please God, must never happen again.

I think I know how it will be.

October 2

J. here every minute he can. Bless him. The greatest kindness in extremis is not nursing, it is mute loving witness. Not what he does, says; that he's there.

It's over, b. No Course Three. Not ever will they say, "she *fought* cancer." This isn't fighting. This is the opposite of fighting. I am the dumb feeble witness to a toxic purge. I succumbed without firing a round.

Where is cure in this? What is left of me whole and well enough to revive?

I take in a little water, rice in broth, nibbles of fruit. I pass unmentionable gruel through scalded passages.

Strength, b. Body no help. The poisons are over. Over, over, over, over. I will think about Brian, fix image after image of him. I will day by day, by grace, prepare for Brian.

October 3

Sports weekend again. J. sent nurse Ritchie to sit with me. I let her go when she got a call saying a Wells player got a concussion. Boy apparently fine now.

Sad somehow that nurse Ritchie knows. Now all Wells knows. Boundaries down, there will be well-meaning trespasses. Don't want that, can't do that. Vital, mobile people make me feel weaker, anxious. But where can I go?

Home is a place where, when you have to go there, they have to take you in . . .

There isn't any place else.

Brian, live this day for Brian.

Sunday, J. home all day. Much better. No church.

First good thing: long reverie, for some reason, about our travels. The curious trip to England when Brian was fifteen to visit literary shrines. Such a pleasure, if a ghostly pleasure, to stand before the inscribed stones of the poets in Westminster. Amid all the fumey clutter and clatter of modern London, the monuments, like the poetry, seemed so majestically accomplished, there forever. Bloomsbury streets, then down south, standing before Jane Austen's desk, up to Yorkshire to the Brontës' house, the moors, Wordsworth's lakes, Hardy's Stonehenge at summer solstice, Chaucer's Bath, Glastonbury where "did these feet in ancient times . . . ." Each called up something like "yes!" or "of course!" from deep headquarters. It made me feel very small yet very happy to make these modest, touristy homages, but my heart broke a little for Brian who seemed, for the most part politely, lost. He had read only a little of the work in school. Through his eyes I know it must have felt like too little to do. Even the hiking, with his mother and dad, in the Lake Country was I am sure a confining—he would have said dorky—thing for a fifteen-year-old boy to endure. He couldn't seem to find food he liked, found "pub lunches" mystifying, bangers and mash an affront, cream teas no kind of treat at all. I could feel his wanting to break out and do something—climb something, take a train somewhere—on his own. Of course he would. I think he liked the shows in London, and he had a pretty diverting afternoon trying to make a punt go forward on the Cam. That was the day he asked us what I thought was such a hopeful question: "How does an American get into a place like Cambridge?" So the fens and water meadows, ancient courtyards and dreaming spires were probably not entirely lost on him. Painful to recall those evening meals, though, when there had been woefully too few "highlights" to exalt in, fiascos to laugh about. It hurt me, and I know J., to feel we were travelling as a family but at the same time failing as a family to make the experience work. Brian I remember kept a journal of the trip. I long to know what he wrote.

The best trip, the magical trip was the following summer doing Switzerland and Italy. This time just J. and I. I was utterly unprepared for such color and light, for the very feel of the air. It too was ancient, its genius already accomplished, but whereas the pleasures of England felt to me like recollections, passing from Switzerland to the

Italian Alps was entirely Other. I must have heard, read, used the word "longing" a thousand times before that summer, but from our balconies overlooking Lake Lucerne and Lake Como, I longed. Pale pink, pumpkin-tinted villas reflected in the ripples of those honey stone lakes. There was something so numinous, so urgent there, I *longed*, I worshipped. I wanted to give up everything, hearth, home, Wells, respectability to wake up every morning on Lake Como. I would have served at table, taken in laundry. I don't know if J. felt it, too. I hope he did. No—I hope he didn't! Wells has been hell enough without a beckoning alternative. We did talk a little about Lake Como being our afterward. Then somehow Little House and the boat got to be the Afterward. Never went again and won't, I'm afraid. Amazing to me how brightly I can still see it.

Second good thing: J. got hold of the P.B.S. videos of *Anna Karenina*, and after a little soup, toast, and chicken bits, we got lost in nearly three hours of it. It is phenomenal how not having a working body heightens one's ability to participate in visual story. Disbelief was totally suspended. I savored every silver hairbrush, every porcelain basin. I loved, in appropriately different senses, all the men. For I of course was the very beautiful, most affecting Anna. Being so insubstantial, I was swept like a butterfly, like a gnat into the wake of her beautiful mess.

I'm very sleepy, b., and I have a taste in my mouth like mustard powder, but I am still thrilled by AK. There is no frigate like a video. Maybe I'm not dead yet. Love you.

October 5

So lightheaded and wobbly on my feet. Cancer and its poisons aside, how could a body stoke itself to rise, walk about, see and think clearly with so little real food—without the whole healthy complex that *wants* food, wants anything. Life = desire, in case anybody forgets.

Head full of soot and fog, I made my jittery way down to the kitchen in late a.m. to address the folder of *Wells Quarterly* proofs. For an eternity it seemed I sat there looking at the folder and my two red pens. Then lugubriously I begin to shuffle through the articles, not one of them remotely interesting to me. There is a deadline, no less—day after tomorrow. Firing on any cylinders at all I could do this work in ninety concentrated minutes. This a.m. no cylinders churn; they sit corroding in their sleeves. I pick up my pen—sheer deadening will—scratch, scratch, scratch.

I don't think I've made much of a mark as a worker. Funny, I always felt like a dynamo of productivity as a student, and I suppose if J. had not married me and carried me off to Milton Academy, I would have finished graduate work in Eng. Lit. and probably taught it somewhere. No regrets about that, I think. The more I have seen of life, granted from pretty remote hide-outs, the less I think of academics and academic life. For every ten thousand tenure-track college professors, there may be two or three true scholars. They're probably both Jesuits. The rest turn out more and less serviceable text books and secondary material and contribute to journals which exist only so that people who are professionally obligated to publish their "research" have a place to put it. Probably a hundred of the ten thousand are also superb teachers, an attainment that usually serves to put less gifted colleagues on edge. Inside their "fields," university-level academics can only, and to a limited extent, talk to themselves. Outside their fields, they can be almost imbecilic, baffled by and suspicious of commerce, usually unable to make mechanical things work, arrogantly sure of themselves on political matters. Most of them hold views on the leftward margins of American liberalism, and they are so cocooned in like-mindedness that they mistake their unexamined assumptions for objective truth. With a tiny bit of reflection they might see that they are liberal-left because that political and economic point of view is the only one that likes universities as they have evolved. Academics don't like authority, even when it is necessary and right. They don't like their chairmen, their deans and provosts, the president or trustees. They tend to see their community, state, and nation as larger, stupider universities, and, correspondingly, academics don't like civil authorities, legislatures, high courts and presidents. Academics are therefore not very good citizens, but they tend to feel they are the best citizens, like Socrates. In their unreliable citizenship academics are a lot like artists, but without the saving grace of art. And I have no doubt whatsoever that if John Greeve hadn't whooshed me off to Milton as I was inching toward orals and thesis at Cornell, I would have joined the legions of university academics, staking out my own fussy claim to something like Women Poets in the First Quarter of the Twentieth Century (or Edna St. Vincent Millay and anybody else I could find to like). Didn't want it, don't miss it. Not that I was asked.

But such a shamefully tiny contribution! I have barely worked. Maybe the nicest part was tutoring the younger, weaker writers at Milton. I remember charging five dollars an hour, more, I consoled myself, than a babysitter gets, except babysitters get more hours. I think I was a good tutor. Or maybe it was that Milton students were so generally sound that the weaker ones were just fine. In English I never saw much difference between the weakest and the strongest, either at Milton or Wells. Almost all of them, bless them, read what they were asked—interesting books generally: *Great Expectations, Jane Eyre, Catcher in the*

Rye. Moreover, I have to say, most of the assigned papers I thought were interesting: How did Jane Eyre's Lowood education prepare her for the world beyond? Were Pip's expectations finally great? Was Holden Caulfield disturbed, or especially sane? So far as I could see even the dimmest fifteen- and sixteen-year-old boys of Milton's boys' division liked thinking about those questions, thought about them rather well. The only things my tutees lacked were strategy and polish, and I believe I helped them on that score. The trick I always felt was to keep it bone simple. "This paper," I would say, "involves making a list and then writing it up." Simple as that. Then we made up the "list"—passages that showed the formative incidents in Jane Eyre's schooling, then the ones that showed how well she got through her adult trials—and presto! The paper was in the bag. Just write up that list, boy-o. The polish came a little harder, since most boys in my experience don't care about polish. Once they think they've seen the point, they lose interest. Standard written English was regarded as at best annoyingly required, at worst merely decorative. But here too, chirpy Mrs. Greeve was good and simple: any damn fool can write a clear, correct sentence, Chip. That's all the essay is, a string of sentences. But in practice it was not so simple when a boy had no conception of, or language for, sentence components, parts of speech. Even then, progressive junior high schools were skipping systematic instruction on the conventions of

English grammar—in favor of what? Building little villages, replicas of Viking ships. "This sentence has no subject" or "Verb and subject don't agree here" create only bewildered sadness in a child who has never experienced the empowering distinction of subject and predicate, noun and verb. But we polished away, those nice lumpy Milton boys and I. Who knows. I think the good part was that I liked them, and they knew it. Faculty were pleased. J. and I used the money for symphony tickets. I guess that was a job, although it didn't feel like one.

Being assistant, then associate, librarian to the Adrian Bourne Library of Wells School felt like a job, although I'm sure everyone knew I was mainly John's tag-along. It felt like a job because I was expected to show up at specified times and got paid mid-month like other Wells staff. Just drifting downstream. Ordering, within the budget, new requisitions, not from passionate hunches and convictions, but after guarded consideration of what library journals recommended and what the few interested faculty cared to suggest. Indexing and cataloguing the books and periodicals as they arrived. I believed it would be nice to work with the boys on research projects, but the occasion was rare. Wells faculty didn't assign much research. When a boy needed help on Islamic fundamentalism or the crack-up of the Soviet Union, Wells' few thousand volumes almost never filled the bill, and inter-library loans from the university at

Storrs were always a little cumbersome. Now with computers, it will all be different. All the texts and data in the world with a few taps and clicks. But it takes a discerning mind to make even basic sense of it all. How does a Wells boy know when to stop the flow? Who will tell him this bit is important and true; this flashy, easy bit false? This bit true, but small; this bit huge. This bit is a conclusion, derived from some other undisclosed source; this bit is the source. When computer screens have the authority of texts and when the texts are too numerous to contend with, what will a Wells boy do? He will skim the flashier bits, he will try to put the whole business behind him.

I would be of no help, not that I ever faced the problem in the Bourne Library. I have never had any interest in All the Information There Is, only in the selected fragments that have by chance or deep destiny printed themselves on my heart. I felt almost deceptive sitting at my librarian's post. I am bookish, and my rooms have always been heaped with books, so a library would seem the most natural setting imaginable for me. But the library was only camouflage, Wells' little gesture toward All the Knowledge There Is. My books at home are secret Meg documents, dark and exciting alchemical texts, books like fires which, when I put them aside, still kindle and bubble, in case I witchily wish—oh! "Witchily wish"—to "do" something with them. My books are like the dangerous kinds of drugs, promising sex, transcendence, ecstatic possibility. I have lived dangerously in my books. The library felt like a benign prison, heavy with safety. And truth be told, I was lonely in there. It was not just that by any measure the stately new fake Georgian building was under-used by the boys. Libraries expect occupants to sit quietly paying no attention to anyone else. One goes to a library to become unrelated. When Brian was an underformer he came in once or twice, and my heart soared, and then he never came at all.

I can still feel the acute awfulness of standing at the checkout desk, peering through the grey light of winter afternoon across the length of the library. If there were one or two heads visible at remote tables, it made the room all the lonelier. I was doing, I realized, absolutely nothing. I was hanging around, waiting, and if I wasn't careful, I was going to realize this in all its force, and then the hiss I was holding at bay just beyond my ears was going to mount to a roar, and I was going to collapse inward to the final hell. Standing useless and without desire at the checkout desk, I was dying in full, unbearable consciousness.

I quit that afternoon. For appearance's sake and not to reflect too badly on J., I took on "other duties": copy editing the *Wells Quarterly,* my alleged eagle eye for the textual error leading to other copy- and proof-reading jobs as they came up. Bearable. The important thing was that I was *out,* escaped, able to breathe a little.

J., who has a knack for the sudden loving gesture, told me one evening out of the blue that the faculty thought I was a "remarkable woman." I told him that Lizzy Borden and Christine Keeler were remarkable women, but I knew what he meant. He wanted me to know that some of his colleagues, who were always wonderfully kind and I think a little afraid of me, thought I was awfully smart. No one would utter the dark formula, but I knew what it was. Intentionally and visibly withdrawing from school life, when the very ethos of the place was to participate, contribute, sacrifice beyond reason, opened up the dawning possibility that there was a great, possibly superior, Other World, and Margaret Greeve seemed to dwell in it. Retreating from Wells made me exotic and strangely important to the community. This is not what J. meant by passing on the "remarkable" compliment. He was speaking, if I recall, of the response to a snippy but pretty effective Op. Ed. piece I had just had published in the daily NYT: "Using, Not Playing, Your Head," about the mental power derived from detaching a child's nervous system from anything that narcotically or electronically moves it, so that *it* can begin to act on the world. Many offers to reprint. I got, in sum, a little less than a thousand dollars. This piece, combined with my three published lyrics (Edna imprisoned in a Connecticut village) in the "This Singing World" column of the *Hartford Courant*, are my entire literary *oeuvre*.

That and you, b.

Still, I would like to have earned my keep. I hope loving J. has helped him to earn our keep. Good, though, to be low impact, no?

Some rest now. Bathe, collect myself. J. home at seven.

October 6

Oh, b., not feeling well at all. It's up and down my chest and belly. The worst is that I can't tell what's discomfort and what is an anxious mood. Perhaps they are one. All night and all morning like a current or buzz: wrong, wrong, wrong.

J. and I will drive to Hartford tomorrow for scans and tests to see what the chemo is accomplishing. Brain is so feeble and my horizon so near I can't imagine caring what they find. I don't even want to ride in the car an hour each way, although I know J. spent time he could ill afford arranging the appointments in Hartford instead of Mass. General. Will my spirit soar if they look at the pictures and say, "Amazing. Not a trace of –*noma* to be seen anywhere!" What would be the meaning of that finding while I am held fast in this sickening hum? Where exactly is my spirit, anyway? Seems to be lying awfully low. Can't imagine it soaring, or even peeping.

Just read over yesterday, b., and I am ashamed of

myself. The puffed up diatribe against academics—who was that speaking, and what on earth does she know about university life? If it took ten thousand aspiring scholars to produce two immortally good ones, and if that were gong on continually, we would have all the scholarship we could ask for. And if the work of some is mulch for others, God bless the whole garden. And as for "a hundred superb teachers"—what a blessing.

So clear that my sour braying is only about me, not about academic life. I was no doubt fleshing out the kind of colleague/scholar/teacher I would have been had I stayed on the treadmill. No one is quicker to inflate than old Meg Greeve. Weak, sick, useless, and immobile, she rattles her one last rusty saber, her overvalued, by-default habit of cerebration at a whole thriving world of men and women who have done her no harm. No more of that, please.

In a suitably penitent spirit, I finished the *Quarterly* copy and called to have it picked up.

I must set myself to sleeping, or at least resting. Also quarts and quarts of water. Surely good clean water will flush the rot away, a Kelseyan image I rather like.

J. home at six, then gone till 8:30 or 9. Hope I can rally for the rest of *Anna Karenina*. Actually, arriving at nightfall, the night table lamps on, and J. moving about the room are all I want.

October 8

The new killer word is "mass." There are still masses in me, whether mere husks or still cooking, where esophagus meets gut, where gut meets intestines, hunkered up against uterine wall, very faintly staining the Cape Horn of one lung. My brain is still clear, and while nobody mentions it, one of my pamphlets suggests this might be the way to go. Quickest and least painful. But would I have to go mad? Would I randomly speak out to world figures long dead? Would J. murmur an endearment to me and would I bark like a dog? Don't want that. Glad my brain is not massive.

The idea, as we discussed before the chemo, is to zap the masses with x-ray. These at least will be quick and painless and can be administered in a clinic near Wells. Compared to the chemo, x-ray side effects should be a piece of cake, although Dr. Dietrich suggested I may feel "a little punk." I asked whether that meant *altogether* a little punk or whether I would be adding another small increment to the all-being total punkness I already feel. Dr. D. appeared bewildered by my question. He said, among other things, that I might feel dehydrated, weak, and that food might not taste right. He was more than bewildered.

J. asked the good questions. Before rising to leave, I had to ask, with what I hoped was bluff good nature, "so how am I doing?" He was utterly expressionless. Then he said that the best sign is that there was no new growth or involvement. He said he was concerned that there is so little reduction in the tumors. This, he told me again, is what the radiation is for.

Riding home to Wells, it settled upon me with great clarity that Dr. D. had not offered any hope. That, I realized, is what must be behind physicians' reputations for coldness and insensitivity in dire circumstances. There is probably no special lack of warmth or empathy; when they know perfectly well the picture is hopeless, warmth is an imposture, and empathy would be unbearable. If they loved you, they would embrace you and conceal the terrible truth. If they are physicians, they state and restate the data and related protocols.

Proceeded quietly to Wells, reconciled to hopelessness, feeling actually a little better.

Quick cup of tea at schoolhouse—herbal for me, real for J.—before he headed back to the office. Alone, I feel like reading something vague and majestic, maybe

125

Marcus Aurelius or Boethius. Then the prospect makes me laugh out loud. Instead I reach for Alice Munro's collected stories, hoping that I have forgotten them enough to love them again. But so sleepy. Sorry b.

October 9

Feeble again today, b., so I may have to peter out soon.

This a.m. I overcame an unexplainable aversion and started into the Kelsey books again. At the heart of it I think was a desire to know if they ever reclaimed someone with prospects dim as mine. Looking hard for the worst cases, I found some pretty dramatic messes, including a few who had turned to the Kelseys after surgeries, but each of them seemed to see the Kelsey light much earlier in their diagnosis and treatment. There was nobody I could find in the done-all-they-can-do-medically dept. Also, nobody who came to them after chemo. Maybe the chemo zaps, along with everything else, your curative essences. Nice thought. Nevertheless I found myself warming again to the idea of addressing illness soulfully and gently. It is now not sounding silly to me at all to wonder about being perhaps nicer to my tumors. Such thoughts before Courses One and Two would have been sheer wishful thinking and cowardice, but now I think I've fairly earned my right to think such thoughts. I can conceive of my body undoing a tumor. I can conceive of soothing myself to a point where benign, restorative forces within me were liberated for the good. Unfurling. Healing should feel like an unfurling.

Everything good in my life, everything deep and transforming and astonishing has felt like an unfurling. There is never any hurrying a true unfurling, only witness and wonder . Crystal Foote, for instance. Crystal Foote! Amazing to think that was—sixteen years ago, when I was forty. Sixteen years since an unfurling. Now if you'll excuse me I have to go get my forties book-ys to see just what unfurled.

B.! I was on fire. And how snippy I was, even then, having fun with the name Crystal Foote, which was and is absolutely the best name for an ethereal yoga teacher. I see that I fantasized about her deep into the night. Dark, lithe beauty in her black leotard, sitting straight backed and pretzel legged in lotus position. In my fantasy then, at least in the dead of night, white-diamond light flashed from a crystal foot.

I seem to have got onto yoga matter-of-factly enough. Val had been yammering on and on about it during our August cruise on the Valmar. She was rhapsodizing miracles on yoga's behalf, and I felt obligated to talk her down to earth. How come, I asked her, if it's hard and even hurts, that it's so restful? And if it's so restful, why is it so energizing? And if it's only restful, what's wrong with a good, no-guilt nap? Val was sweet to ignore these nigglings. She really wanted to share yoga with me, and the good will struck deep, because after all my sophistry and ribbing, I went home and went on the prowl for a yoga class.

The Wellness Center in Kent, when I visited, was about as suggestive of the mysterious east and deep inner knowing as the Stop 'n Shop. But there were, as advertised, four yoga classes per week, and the instructor was Crystal Foote. Crystal was beautiful almost to the point of being disturbing—and it wasn't only me. She was rather tall, 5'7" or 5'8", and she had wonderful, shiny honey-brown hair worn long and straight, to about her bottom, except for class when she did it up in a stylish twist, somehow arranged in about two seconds around something like a chopstick. In book-y 81 I see I referred to Crystal as a "colt," and I can remember deciding reflexively that she was too thin, then realizing that she wasn't. She was instead light, wonderfully light. She moved lightly, she was light on her long brown feet. Willed and forced thinness always betrays itself in harsh, worrying concavities, an effect of ravaged scrawniness. Not so with Crystal Foote. Arms and legs were both slender and somehow full. Her belly was flat and her waist seemed tiny—although she had two babies under four.

No cosmetics could create the rosy flesh along her jaw line. Crystal Foote was, and no doubt still is, beautiful in a way that has always made me want to give up trying. Straightforward and sweet as she was, it was an effort at first not to resent her.

And then there was the yoga. My skepticism lasted about a minute. Even when I couldn't bend where Crystal bent in the early sessions, I was rapt. I loved my little rubber mat. I came to love everything. There were usually about eleven or twelve of us, a gaggle of women in their thirties and forties—and one man, Lonnie. Lonnie was doughy and bulky and in the months I observed him at yoga, he never seemed to be able to do anything at all, the configurations of his hulking arms and legs in no relation whatsoever to the positions Crystal demonstrated. He was always idiotically cheerful. In the closing silence and meditation, he usually fell asleep, his deep, troubled inhalations and exhalations a bearable distraction. Who would have guessed that Lonnie could surface again in consciousness?

It did not take me long to become devoted to the yoga and to Crystal. It was more than a little hypnotic, and it also felt, as Val said it would, wonderfully invigorating. Such a wonderful, wonderful feeling of time, that is, no time passing. The sessions were ninety minutes, including the closing meditation. It could have been a minute, or hours. Every cliché about yoga is true. One *is* "in" the moment, every moment. One *is* "in" her body. I was in my body. I was also, it turned out, mighty supple. Yoga! I can't begin to imagine, lying up in this bed festooned with friendly old book-ys, how I managed to get so far from my body. Could a dedicated yogi ever get cancer? Is there a yet retrievable yogic principle for me? Hard to imagine.

But there was, when I was forty, that definite unfurling, and it wasn't yoga itself; it was more what the yoga allowed. It wasn't also, entirely, Crystal, but she was an angel to unfurl to. I don't think I quite knew, and certainly never named, what was happening. It was good enough just to feel it. But I was falling in love with Crystal Foote. If I had been a little more finely tuned, I would have realized that I was also picking up the currents and undercurrents of the whole class, excepting possibly Lonnie. Everyone was in love with Crystal, in love with the love of Crystal, with the slow, yogic extensions of that love. How could you not be? The beautiful bones of that face, dark hair, bright dark eyes, the balletic perfection of her movements. Her movement was a kind of language. Of course I moved to it, compliant, worshipful. Of course it was sexual. I don't think I really fantasized about "running off to the Caribbean with Crystal"—although that light aside (from Feb. book-y 82) would turn out a little prophetic. The combination of my eyes swimming attentively all over Crystal's perfect leotarded body and my own serenely invigorating exertions released terrific libido. "A new, or recovered(?) Sapphic impulse in Mrs. Greeve?" I noted (also Feb. 6. 82). Didn't really trouble me, actually never has. It was altogether invigorating. Brian was oblivious, but J. knew something was up. I was becoming positively venturesome and frisky in bed; J. pleased as could be. Nice all around, I think, but as I said, I should have been more respectful of the currents.

Of course all that new libido, the whole unfurling, would have to go somewhere. Several of us yogists had become rather tight, were meeting before and after classes for tea and talk. We felt smug and good and cultic about what we felt but could barely bring ourselves to name. To me, and I am sure them, more time with yoga friends felt like more time in the yoga feeling, more Crystal time. Talk came up of other "body work," deep breathing, massage, group aerobics. I was, we were, for all of it. Three or four of us, sometimes with Crystal, sometimes on our own or at Devon Bemish's house, would get together and breathe deeply in sync for a half hour or more, until one or all of us was thoroughly altered. I remember being afraid and then fascinated when my fingers grew stiff and curled in tetany and Crystal saying no, no, it was fine, it was supposed to happen; breathe through it, breathe, breathe. Devon would get to a point where she would sob convulsingly, and we would hold her to us and rock her. We were, we believed, getting "clear" of traumas and blocks held in the soma, prior to consciousness. That's what I see now, us standing in various pairs, breathing rhythmically, looking in each other's eyes, perhaps clasping hands, occasionally embracing, perfectly glad to open up to what kept unfurling.

J. home—it's dinner time, and I've been sitting up here since noon. Best day since cancer. Back to unfurling tomorrow? Legs all pins and needles. Come up, come up, lovely J.

October 10

Clinic this a.m. for my silent zaps. Radiologist and technician girl good, I think. We waste no time. My wretched masses are in such a variety of parts of me, I have to get into the damndest positions for them to line up the targets in their sites. Astonishing that they can focus their killer rays with such pinpoint accuracy. At least I hope they can. Click, hum, "all right, Mrs. Greeve, now if we can—" All under the brightest, yellowest fluorescence.

Home by ten, and J. off to school. Another endless mess, he tells me, not really wanting to tell me. A wayward boy brought LSD to school and was caught distributing it to some friends, all to be sacked. J. sees it as a Sisyphean boulder. He has to help the boys involved make sense of the deed, then the school, and of course he has to break the parents' hearts. At least one of them is being venomous about it and is talking about suing, so J. has to negotiate with the board and with school lawyers. He doesn't have to say that in the aftermath of every bigger-than-usual stink, the school's collective mood dips to the floor, with the usual projective charges of inequity, inept handling, soft-headedness/lack of compassion. Enough of these and the invisible black banner of Bad School is hoisted ominously above the campus. All J.'s fault, all his to bear. Too often, b., I have hated what this school and this work have done to him. Day after day, night after night he goes back to it.

This morning I was thinking about the boys, one of whom, Marc Slavin, a diminutive ferret of a boy, I got to know a little. What would he have been thinking and feeling in anticipation of getting hold of his own little lick of LSD? Was it the outlaw rush of acquiring it? The rumored epic distortions and disorientation of the trip? He obviously, all delinquency and pudding-headedness aside, wants more of something. More what? What are the real rumors, boy-to-boy, that make the risk so irresistible? Is it a hoped for, instant unfurling, a short cut to that? If that's it or even part of it, however unsafe or unwise of the boys, I understand it.

Yesterday's unfurling. So, so strange to go back there again, to Crystal, Devon, and the girls. The yoga, the breathing bouts, feel, touch. It wasn't quite a year, but it seems a distinct epoch of life. Center of gravity shifted from Wells to Kent, though there was no real betrayal of J. I don't remember even feeling a concern about that. Devon was just divorced, and some of the

other women were not too firmly rooted in their outwardly conventional families, but J. and I were elemental,
deeply safe, a good place to unfurl from.

And unfurl I did. We all did. Devon, who seemed to
have money, managed to get me to a spa she went to where
we were massaged with silken hands at a heavenly tantric
pace that carried me past any sense of time. There too I was
tanned by bright lamps while lying naked in a closed metal
cylinder. I was shampooed, facially wrapped and, once,
made over. J. was incredulous, also stirred(!). In the course
of massage, which was almost sex, tapes were played of
rising and falling gusts of wind, breaking waves. Scents,
light incenses, aromatic oils. Yes, yes, yes to all of it.

With Devon, now my best, best friend, it was more
than almost sex. Devon was herself studying massage. She
practiced Shiatsu and another wondrous kind in which
the masseuse's hands don't even touch the subject's
body; they move intuitively along the spine and other
planes of flesh, transmitting, eliciting putative "energies."
One late a.m. after yoga and yoga tea, Devon asked me
over for lunch. She wanted to give me a massage, which
I thought was wonderful. She would in the weeks ahead
indeed give blissful, ultimate massages, but that first one
was disrupted and overwhelmed by other impulses.
Probably because we had wine for lunch. Not just one
chilly glass, its water-beaded bowl dangerously full over
its skinny stem, but two.

Devon spread a comforter on the floor of her spare bedroom, covered the comforter with a sheet. I undressed and lay out on the sheet. She went off and when she returned with arms full she looked down at me and said, "Oh, look at you." As a person to be massaged, I assumed an attitude of silent compliance. Devon drew the shades, placed candles in little bowls at the perimeter of the sheet. A tape was inserted, some kind of white noise and then a flute, barely audible. Devon knelt beside me. I heard her moistening her hands with oil, and then the good surprise of her hands on the small of my back.

Happily, unfurlingly lost. When it was time to turn over, I was very torpid and slow from the wine and touching and darkness. I noted that Devon too had taken off her clothes, the candle light creaming her white breasts in contrast to the tan of her midriff. No surprise at all then that after a tensing minute or so I was touching her, too, ecstatic, starved for it. Absolutely, absolutely. Oh *yes*, I thought, and oh yes, I said, and then it was no longer massage, but sex, new but also not new. Utterly affirming, no edges, no urgency, the best kind of opening up and exploring. I was pleasuring Devon extravagantly—belly, fingertips, my toes along the expanse of her calf—but I was not primarily engaged with her. I was swimming, now really unfurling in the buoyant, yielding medium of this lovely sex.

B., as God is my witness, there was no guilt, not

while we scissored and caressed, stroked and slid, or afterward driving home to Wells, or at dinner, or in bed. Whatever Devon wanted from me, she seemed to have gotten. She was the same sweet, loopy Devon when we embraced at my car, as when we first poured out those chilly glasses of Chardonnay. "Lesbian, lesbian, lesbian, lesbian," I see I wrote in March, b.82, then "I don't really think so, no." Bisexual then? I suppose so, on the evidence, but the obvious and affirming fact of the matter was that I felt utterly the same, fundamentally unaltered, just more realized in the body department, and in Deep Meg, decidedly and thrillingly unfurled.

But not at all life-changing. Devon and I had each other perhaps a half dozen more times, each of them at least tenuously related to the yoga/bodywork dream. After the first marvelous secret time, I remember rising at the end of yoga meditation as Crystal made her way to my mat. She clasped both my hands and looked into my eyes without speaking. Then at last she said, "You're doing well, aren't you?" Could she tell? Would Devon have told her? Were they that close? I gave Crystal such a hug.

That spring a few weeks after, it all fell apart; rather it flew south. Crystal, who was married, or possibly partnered, to a man who was developing a new fitness apparatus, told us one morning that she was moving to Key West. She spoke to us very deliberately, as if to acknowledge she was dealing out more than a routine emotional blow. She was, as reasonably realized women usually are, aware that a complex relationship of some weight had come to be. She was its center, and she knew it. As she outlined the availability of other yoga classes in the region, the whole good dream seemed to float off like a bubble. I didn't know if I was sad. I remember hoping that I would stay unfurled. Alone I think among the inner circle I was unaware that a group migration was already planned. Devon and three others were following Crystal to Key West, families be damned in two cases. Afterward, it left a bad, though highly localized, mark, almost a scandal. Opinions were voiced and even printed in Kent that something unsavory had occurred at the Wellness Center. There were suggestions of feminism darkly and seductively at work, a feeling that women idle enough to assemble at will and otherwise indulge body and whim were not good for the community. Yoga, as the common practice linking the women making their sudden exodus, was vilified to the extent that classes were not resumed at the Wellness Center.

Just like a bubble rising into bright sky and disappearing. Off flew my yoga and Crystal and funny, silky Devon and that gift of lightness itself which visited me without asking when I was 40.

I always believed I would tell J. about it, really about it, Devon especially. The lovely thing is that I always could. Few of J.'s friends or colleagues understand him well enough to know that he could hear it, hold it, take it deeply in, let it deepen us. No unfurling would diminish me for him. That is your great, great goodness to me, J. You have always wanted me unfurled. Have I ever for a second been that generous? I am afraid not.

No earthly point in telling him now.

He will be home soon. I must divert him, as I hear the discipline flap over the LSD is bad as it gets—gloom, board mess, and lawyers. Rise to it, Meg. Grow, hair! Maybe some videos.

October 11

Not at all right today. Standing up from the bed I almost fell over. Mouthful of sour ashes. Try again later, B.

Later. Think I'll just lie here and let the world, if there is one, fold in on me. Val called late a.m., so comfortable, so sweet. She really does make me feel all's right with the world, always has. Odd how I listened to my voice telling her about x-rays, my prescriptions, peeing fire and other symptoms, and I sound sure of myself, summon up extra force in my voice. The woman talking to Val on the phone was in control, nothing to worry about. As soon as I hung up, my stomach was all fluttery, and I was perspiring through my nightie. It occurs to me what a physically expensive thing it is to be "managing well." Poor darling J.

Later still. Arnold is lumbering around downstairs doing about the perpetually running toilet in the powder room. How hard can it be to repair or replace? Surely Arnold has attended to it thirty or forty times since we've lived here. Arnold is always extremely gloomy about the prospect of anything wrong improving. The powder room toilet seems to share his karma. In a peculiar way the whole campus does. Why do I find this *reassuring*, and why do Arnold's footsteps below—even the footsteps conveying muffled pessimism and doubt—make me want to laugh out loud? Is it because I know that, however improbable and grotesque, Arnold Leiber likes me? It is.

Four p.m. Arnold gone at last. I teeter down for tea in the kitchen. I am tempted to flush the powder room toilet, but pass it by superstitiously.

Pleasant cup, rereading yesterday in b. Interesting from a day's distance. It was unfurling, certainly, but what a strange thing simply to have arisen and departed. There was so little resonance or even dissonance with everything else in my life at the time, Brian, Wells, propriety, whatever I may have thought I was when I was 40.

I suppose I should not be surprised, especially now that I have this Alamo perspective, that the deep truths one stumbles upon are always uncomfortable, inappropriate, beyond polite social category. Civilization may be, as Freud thought, bearable neurosis, unavoidable, tragic compromise. Soul and survivable good sense forever at war. And how did my Edna know this so eloquently?

So subtly is the Fume of life designed,
To clarify the pulse and cloud the mind . . .
. . . . the poor treason
Of my stout blood against my staggering brain,
I shall remember you with love, or season
My scorn with pity—let me make it plain:
I find this frenzy insufficient reason
For conversation when we meet again.

Why are we born if our situation in life has already
been sorted out and perfectly framed by others? I suppose
I did season my scorn with pity in Devon's case. Her letters from Florida were appalling, unreadable, as are so
often the written utterances of those we come to know in
other ways. She would actually inscribe "apropos of
nothing at all" and "anyhoo" and "☺," "☺." And our
frenzy was clearly insufficient for conversation if we met
again. We never did.

Upstairs for a sleep before J. On the way, tried the
powder room toilet. Still running.

October 13

Very bad yesterday. Burning cramps above and below my belly. The x-rays doing their job? Not doing their job? Went in yesterday a.m. for more clicks and hums. Very uncomfortable, and I was, I'm afraid, sour with the technician.

Home and back to bed. Shallow sleep penetrated with sickening regularity by searing cramps in the belly.

This morning the same. Nothing diverts. T.V. awful.

October 14

Very bad in my guts, frightened.

Went to clinic this a.m. for x-rays. Belly now bloated, too tender even to touch. Radiologist concerned, called Dr. D. at Mass. General. A scan is ordered, dye in my veins, awful metallic taste in my throat.

Verdict: something is stopped up where stomach meets intestines. There was a "mass" there—at the ileum?—to begin with, but now it's blocked, and food is not moving along. Dr. Henkel the radiologist says it could be "electrical" or in the valve itself. I don't understand "electrical," don't care, only want pain and pressure to go away. The food stuck in my gut is apparently putrefying to gas and other unthinkable degradations. I can't, don't want to, think of solutions. If my cancer has damaged the valve, is digestion forever over? It is all I can imagine. I am Arnold at the powder room toilet. No solution, never has been. That kind of world.

Hurts too much.

Back to my bed after two nights in hell at the clinic.

Stimulated by medicines, I finally passed the foetid mess in my sealed-off stomach. Things not all right. Ileum not only cancer-involved, but apparently torn up. Cancer's fault? Treatment? Who knows. I'm not to eat "solid food," as if I had steak and corn on the cob in mind. If this is the way it will go, with unbearable, white-hot cramps where tummy and womb were, then give me the black capsule. Must never, never have that again.

Serious-pain meds now. Take me way down a well, then float up above what I sense dimly is the same acrid distress, but eerily disconnected from mattering.

Before I was wheeled out to the car, I hear Dr. H. tell J. there will be only one more session of radiation, but not for the ileum. I want this to be good news. No more Hitler in the bunker, but I don't know, I can't think straight or feel much at all.

My own bed, though. My own bed.

October 17

A small but still very welcome victory as I hunker back into the narrowing recesses of this cave: I can actually read while looped on my new morphia. Utterly unworldly. My body feels like a boneless swimmer in some, I must say, rather agreeable medium, and when I try to think through an in-this-world plan like going to the shelves in the good guest room for a certain book, it all seems staggeringly confusing. But I open a book, concentrate a little, and I can proceed vividly ahead, wonderfully abstracted from my physical husk with its half dozen no doubt vengeful embers.

Most of the morning lost in Powell's *Dance to the Music of Time*, my favorite volume of it, *At Lady Molly's*. Nobody can do what Powell does to me. I get *history*, an entirely other history than my own, but as real, no realer. Joyce's and Woolf's interior time isn't real time. It's interesting, but it's actually frenetic, hopped up. Powell's people, a whole circus of them, move in real time. There is the right amount of uncertainty and then surprising coming together, lots of hilarious acting-out of people's unsheddable habits and obsessions: Uncle Giles booking his room at the Ufford in anticipation of a family reconsideration of "the trust," wonderful/horrible Widmerpool pushing himself ploddingly and monstrously forward in the world, exquisitely balanced by a fleeting glimpse of beautiful Stringham receding another degree into dipsomania. Lots of parties in Powell, but parties with no momentum, just big unlikely structures in which characters are fated to connect. And sweet, modest Nick taking all of it in and telling it all in his stuttering, yet pitch-perfect syntax. All great writers who work in real world, real time have to be terrifyingly, ruinously honest. Despite what seems like crippling reserve, Nick is honest that way. He is honest about the central, hardest thing, his own loneliness, the exact distance from each character he touches or almost touches, needs or dreads. Of course it is a comic masterpiece. Algerian wine drunk out of chipped cups in a painter friend's grimy studio, dark pints and desultory chatting at down-at-heel pubs, donning evening clothes in the gloom of a dingy bachelor flat, to Lady Molly's where the variegated misfits are greeted by slovenly manservants, the carpets again rolled back for dancing. Is there an era of my own life I can feel and recall as acutely—see, smell—as I can London in the twenties, thirties, the Blitz? Not by a mile. Nobody I ever recommended Powell to, except J., liked him a bit. Jake Levin wondered whether I wasn't trying too hard, due to some anglophilic need, to love the unlovable. In short, I was affecting a taste. He went so far even to find an article explaining that British literati don't read AP, only wannabes. Poor Jake, poet or not, he has mainly a tin ear, if not a tin heart. If he did a little homework, he'd find that P's contemporaries read him fervently, including the unpleasable Evelyn Waugh. Powell's angry young critics can't stand that his stoic, majestic, unkillable achievement doesn't move with their febrile currents, didn't come out of that, doesn't depend on that. To chart, seriously, the music of time, you must have a foothold out of time. This is why, deceptive naturalism aside, AP will certainly stand with the immortals, while the detractors of this age will slide away with the journalists. Oh, AP, I love you, love you for what you have given me, love you so much I don't have the faintest desire to meet you, know you, bother you for a second.

Lunch of beef broth, salad, slices of pear. Not too hard. Another shiny capsule of my morphia. Whoosh down, float up again, then very, very nice. This could be bad, I mean too good. Will Meg Greeve end her days like Coleridge and Thomas de Quincey, in the thrall of morphia? Well down the road to Xanadu? I'll take it over retching myself inside out in a white-sheeted cell in Boston.

And, again, I've been granted books again. AP forever, or when the capacity for real streets and real rooms starts to flag, I can ascend to epic and myth. I can sing in Portia's garden, I can crow and bleed with Clytemnestra. I've always loved the ascent from the grueling particular to the vast and eternal. I remember savoring, positively rolling around in Barbara Tuchman's thirteenth century, then having to get out, way out. Went to—who cares?— Rilke, *Duino Elegies*. Took me right out of this world. I was as trembly and achy as I'll bet he was, reaching after the thing beyond the thing. Edna too, Edna especially— "Euclid alone has looked on beauty bare. Fortunate they who, once only and then but far away, have heard her massive sandal set on stone." Tingles at the back of the neck. What the brain dumbly does at the Presence.

Suddenly, blissfully asleep for two hours, nearly smothered in books and book-y. So *that's* sleep. I remember sleep. Thank you, God, thank you, morphia.

Later. J. home for dinner. Lasagne from the Bryants and salad for him, salad, rice and herbs and apricot juice for me. Wish we could have wine but know better. Still nice to think about wine with J., nice or nicer than wine. J. notes I look rested, better. Actually feeling a little uncertain after the food, but even the memory of feeling better apparently communicates. My last pill has to wait till bed time. We watch a video of Churchill from Dunkirk to V-E day. Even knowing the outcome, I was overwhelmed by the enormity of the effort, not just for WC but for England. All that oppressive action and necessity. Hitler was such a darkness, he must have seemed inevitable. But Churchill stood, like a touching, tenacious Humpty Dumpty, where I know I would have succumbed. Is it cancer or Deep Meg telling me I'm not strong enough for history? I wonder why. I seemed to begin so well. Questions still to be answered. Sleepy now. Come, morphia.

October 18

Cruel surprise. J. drove me to the clinic this a.m. for what was to have been my last radiation treatment. Pictures showed something big and terrible at the base of my stomach, where the trouble was before.

So here I am again in Hartford, imprisoned in white, wired up to fluids. Apparently they need to get at this thing, cut it up, "clear it." I have held firm from the outset that there will be no holding-action surgeries, but they make a case that they can sneak into me with little wiry tubes with even smaller snippers inside the tubes and get at the thing. I'm worn out, b. Let them at me. Let them take me snip by tiny snip. Just let there be morphia.

Poor J. is frantic. He wants to stay, and he has to go, Wells as needy as a big crabby baby. I hate this more for J. than for me.

They will do the snipping in the a.m. I told J. just to call. This will undoubtedly not be the worst. Hell and blast. Where's Rilke? I'm going straight to Rilke, so back off, nurses. No samples or souvenirs for at least two hours. Medicine indeed.

October 21

You don't want to know, b. Snipped into something toxic apparently, and now I am septic all over, septic in my mouth, septic in my teeth. Foul, weak, and dim past caring.

I am a septic product of this septic place. I want the quiet of my own bed. Oh, God, let me go home. This was wrong, I was all wrong about this. These people may all be very nice but they're duly executing their routines. They're dumb about and afraid of anything outside the routines, and they don't even know the cumulative effect of each other's routines, and there's nobody at headquarters directing the one big routine. They are looking away now. I can feel them looking away the way the cowardly waiters do when they know you want them but the food's not ready or there are other things to do. If they looked at me, they would have to face their helplessness.

No good, b., Morphia, sleep. Please home.

October 23

In my bed in school house, and b., between you and me, I am never going back there.

Although I seem to have taken a good portion of the world's medical complex home with me. There is a stainless-steel table stocked with fluids and meds. for me. There is a genuine hospital IV wired, probably forever, into the crook of my arm, there is a wheelchair which I don't believe I need just yet, though it sits there, sculpturally suggestive of an electric chair. Much more imposing is the figure of Nurse McCarty—Connie—who, all shiny in nursey white, sits like an iceberg in J.'s wing chair, unless of course I tell her I don't need her, which I plan to make the rule. Tomorrow a snappy intercom arrangement will be rigged up between here and the guest room, so Connie and, I understand, two or three others, can periodically mop my brow or prepare my pills or pour more goop into the IV. Poor dear J. had to set all this up, which we can probably ill afford. For the present it all makes the room, the house feel like somewhere else to me, although I'm sure in the days ahead I will find it a godsend. No more hospitals, no more trips, except the last one, and there need be no hurry or flashing lights on that occasion.

Reassuring that there's my morphia capsules on the stainless-steel table, and also, I understand, quite a dose included in my IV drip. So I really am a high-tech deQuincey. Glad, glad, glad to be home. J. has been banished from sleeping in here, not that he would want to, with all this clap trap and, no doubt, the heavy mist of pathology and rot hovering over the bed.

They haven't said so in plain language, but my stomach-to-bum digestion is probably wrecked, the "interference" with my ileum making continuing peristalsis "unreliable." Juice, water, gruelly samples of baby food for the foreseeable. My fuel, such as it is, is going to come through the IV. What's to fuel? I'm sure the folks up at the Kelseys' are exhaling deep, piteous sighs on my behalf. Holistic-ier than thou. Bah, humbug. When their ileums go, they'll get strained pears and yogurt. I have sister morphia.

So, b., this is terminal. What do we think? Probably be easier to think once it doesn't feel so transitional. Might Connie or any of the others reveal unsuspected depths or fascinating secrets? Truth to tell, I'm rather hopefully eyeing the television, now wheeled right up to the foot of the bed. I should in my condition be able to skip right over the reflexive squeamishness and plunge wholeheartedly into the horrors, soaps, talk shows, even the outdoors channel which is always broadcasting from some photogenic "wild" quarter to show anxious, kitty-faced predators crouching, hiding, then tearing after helpless prey, nearly always some kind of deer and their babies. Just the way it is in vast majestic Nature. But it is actually worse. The subtext screams that the odds are against all of them, even the head lion. Worse than bad odds, it's over. Their futile cycles of predation are just T.V. now, like—exactly like—the gritty police shows. After T.V., only zoos, then only museums.

Oh, book-y, I am so sick I am now talking sick, seeing the world sick. Surely in a whole other sphere from this sickness and sick room, there are lionhearted, irresistible young Churchills of nature aborning.

Please! J. Due at "supper" time. We will dismiss Connie and hunker here in my tent for a spell. Good, good J. There is still J.

October 24

Woke feeling strangely O.K. Impressive, morphia-in-the-drip.

J. touched my cheek before leaving for school. I did not quite come up from my torpor. Connie reincarnated as Gwen. Gwen has lighter hair, same pulled-back do, same resigned heavy no-ankle legs. She reassures me I can hobble my IV thing-y with me into the bathroom. It has friendly little wheels. Not so bad, medical science.

Arranged rather comfortably, rather regally in bed, free now of Gwen. My head is full of J. This is all very wearing on him, I know. I'm afraid that I and this other formidable entity, my Care, have become something else for him to manage. Cruel and wrong, but he must of course. I will set myself to this, since I have been discharged from all other earthly duties. I will be easy, I will make this easy for him. I will swallow back bile, if I must, sit up straight, and I will engage that beautiful man in a world beyond Wells and cancer. I will make him laugh somehow.

Read, doze, read, doze, Powell's *The Kindly Ones.* Good and darkening, like me. J. popped in mid-a.m. to sit, see how the arrangement is working. Relieved, I think. Wells roars along. All the big Haverhill matches on Sat. I feel J. steeling himself for events. Somehow he will summon up the boom-boom attitude required. Beyond wondering that for boys games have to matter. Go, Wells, go.

Sure of foot, decidedly stooped, and incidentally way too thin, J. plods on uphill, I'm sure he feels, forever. It's the road he knows, the road he chose.

It's also the road we chose. Not merely Wells—in a way, not even Wells. There was plenty of talk and dream, sputter and hope, when we decided to marry. Not decided—realized we were going to marry. Never a doubt. Frank and Val, without a lot of thought, put us together that night at the Indian restaurant on Brattle Street, and poof! It was all very clear. No more scouting and schemes, wondering without hope if something more might be made of Philip Lowenthal. All the other men— what am I saying, boys—I knew were hovering around that set, sure-center J. already was, maybe always was. I knew he was relieved to find me, somehow fatigued by the wait. The first night he loved me he let me know. Walking me back to my Chauncey Street digs in dewy, chirping, disorienting first morning, he said to me, "How is it that there's nothing wrong with you?" I hadn't

159

brushed my teeth. My stockings were in my bag.

I knew exactly what he meant. Before he said it, I knew. I think we both knew. We didn't decide anything; we converged, irrevocably. Road is the right metaphor. We didn't veer onto it, we found ourselves already, always there, now in step.

Thirty-three years on this road together. The prospects along the wayside are brighter and dimmer, but the road is always the road. We made Brian and dandled him in our arms, hoisted him up over our shoulders, led him by the hand, then, bewildered and grave with hope, let him sprint out ahead, linger furtively behind. Turned off somewhere—do they all? Could he, *could* he be waiting up beyond a bend? Is he forever on some other road, his very own road?

The road, the road. Sometimes sunburnt and laughing we were too full of the sights and sounds, our bodies and glad hearts too full to mind the road. Were we once road weary? Never, never were. Sometimes we sailed that road, and once J., in the days of charts and compasses and tide tables, said to me through the gloom of blue fog and anonymous black water, "We could be anywhere." We were, the Valmar a sodden, salt-soaked question mark moving toward any compass point somewhere, we believed, between Freeport and Kittery. Just the road. One time we ascended right out of that fog, so high that everyday atmosphere was fog compared to the light and vivid beauty of the Swiss and Italian lakes. Our road took us there. We arrived on our real legs in our real shoes in a paradise, a myth place that showed itself to us, let us see its paint-pallette villas, fish shimmering like honey and foil under the piers, stones shimmering like fish, geraniums so red orange in their painted boxes on the bridges they seemed to make little shouts at the sun. In the shadows and in rosy dusk, we felt the age of the place and all of its hovering souls. Rousseau, Casanova, Hesse. Forgotten rascals in high boots and cod pieces, muslin-bloused beauties with baskets on their heads. The doors and windowsills cerulean blue, pumpkin orange, forest green. Every tile in its place, every brass hinge richly oiled. In the open market the silver-black flanks of fish, the water-beaded heads of lettuce too alive and beautiful to buy or eat. Carts, donkeys—why, still? Sagging dories and weathered oars. Our road took us there, to Locarno, Lugano, Como. Took us there, and they were waiting for us. Offering us up glasses of wine, baskets of cool plums, steaming trout in buttery sauce. Time slowed, promised, promised to open to an eternity if we would stop, if we would stay. We sat entranced on terraces and balconies in last light of day, wondering at this. We made love on sun-blown sheets with every window wide open to the rush of breeze and the giddy slip-slop of lake on stone. This place, this clear-at-last Locarno was as real as making love, real as each other.

But it was the road. The road was what we trusted. The road was what we knew. Without even knowing it we were back in the grey world again, even when its sun was shining with all its ordinary might. I wonder now: did we belong there? Is that why we arrived? Or were we just to have glimpsed and felt it, so we'd know.

We kept to our road, the road that passed through Wells and keeps passing through. Like swallows sometimes we swoop aside, J. to his conferences and workshops in Princeton or New York, to Sandwich and Little House and a sniff of the sea, and I, my swallow wings dipping obliquely into the still enchantment of books or even, once, to Kent and Crystal Foote and a tremulous unfurling of body and heart, but our arcs criss-cross the road, define it exactly.

No perspective on our road. We are always just where we have arrived, with no view to any place else. It's not just that I'm sick, it's always been that kind of road. We're here, J. and I, only here, this one road just to ourselves. True for me, I know true for J. Surely that is what married means. The only road, the shared only road. This is the deepest, greatest blessing, to have journeyed, to have been one in this way. But is it too cruel finally for the one who is left? Can it be our road without me? Can he travel our road without me, holding the memory of me like a great sack over his shoulder? No, stop, of course not. It is cruel. It's the cruelest fact of all. What—do the two lanes, on that day, narrow to one? Is J. to carry on alone, in his one lane? Is it because I won't see this that I can't see it? Monstrous selfishness in me. But I can't. I can't see J. on that road.

Oh, b., where have I come to? Here, I suppose. Right terribly here.

J., beloved J., with every breath I have left I pledge to cherish, celebrate, and, with God's grace, fortify your precious self.

October 26

Made up my mind to spend a dissolute, utterly self-indulgent day yesterday—not even to spend it, to step aside, let it bubble up and carry me off.

Truth is I fibbed a bit to Connie and took rather more morphia—three times, no less—than I needed. I decided just to see, to lie there in that narcotic soup, off into a dream, then surfacing with ringing ears to a waking reality—light parsed by window mullions—more stupefyingly complex than any dream. Gave up, just lay there, and felt. I now understand addicts perfectly. You give up, say yes to uselessness, and from the deepest, most beckoning place forgive yourself. Terribly, helplessly, you know better. I did that, b. Maybe I am an addict now. Not sure I like that initial spilling-out-the-top-of-my-head feeling.

Feel quite myself today, a sour and sick old bag of bones. I really am a bag of bones. Hard to find a way to scooch up and sit without feeling pelvic bones burning into my pitiful bottom. What a mess.

Will atone for my surely morphia-induced oddness with J. Poor baby was worried about me. I remember telling him with Delphic seriousness: "Talk to Arnold. He knows the truth about Wells." What could I have been thinking of?

Not feeling any special narcotic craving, maybe because it's right here.

I've got to do this better, while I still can. I need to be inventive and if possible interesting to J. Before brain is invaded, before heart clogs, lungs fill, I really must create a delight or two, at least pose fascinating questions.

Real sickness, like analysis, negates. To project sickness faithfully would depress everyone. Sentence has been passed, and there will be no pardon. The doctors, these nurses, J. and I, and possibly Val and Frank know this, but we can still blink an eye, change the subject, drive it out of consciousness as we have practiced since we were children.

Margaret are you grieving
Over Goldengrove unleaving?

Never was. Grieving only for myself. Strange, awful terrain if I open my eyes wide. I am moving toward it, and it is moving toward me. Its image is a storm, a dark, lowering storm, but when this storm engulfs you, it darkens and cancels you and you die. To its approach I feel a manageable, workaday, only slightly cowardly dread. At those instants—five, six times a day—when its certainty makes a flash behind my eyes and takes my breath away, I know my soul is having a brush with the ultimate. The feeling is sickening in the vicinity of my ruined stomach and also a feeling I am about to cry. I come so close, so close, but I don't seem to let go.

I will not bow, at least yet, to this negation. I will be bright. I will scan my deep interior for images. I will think on brightness, dwell only in brightness. Help me, b. For J. God help me.

October 27

This morning I lighted on a summer night in Lincoln when I was seven or eight. School over and far from beginning. Dusk has fallen more quickly than I expected, and I step from behind our garage when I had managed to clear skunk cabbage and burdock and, with such indescribable satisfaction, to dig a hole for something, possibly a grave. Stepping away from my secret, archaic project, I saw that darkness had smoked over the back lawn, and fireflies like hovering messengers were glowing and blackening over the dark hedges. Beyond our yard there was all the lush business of a summer night, the slosh of bicycle tires slowing over the warm pavement, the sock of a hard ball into an oily leather glove, a little crescendo of laughter from a distant porch, the final squeals of play. Dark now, but with some green still showing in the greys, the street was wonderfully settled, benignly complex. There were secrets everywhere but also a vast encompassing realm where all the secrets were known. I was alone at the far end of my dark lawn, rapt, aware of a pattern in all of it, yes a pattern, and I was part of it. My first intimation, I think, of history.

Me: all alone at the far end of a darkening garden.

October 29

Very uncomfortable. Pressure like a dry ball wedged between my diaphragm and breastbone. Breathing shallow. Same no matter what position I lie in. Can I have grown a great ball in my chest overnight? Please be gas, and pass.

I will rise above this. I will dwell for a time in the dunes, the whole moonscape world of dunes between Truro and Provincetown. I was nine or ten. One of the few sentences I can remember from my father: "This is land's end, Meg. This is the end of the world." Dunes at the end of the world. There was one brilliant beach day near the Race Point light. I slipped away from the family blanket and skittered up over the rise of dunes into a pure arcadia of sand forms, hillocks, hollows, crags and crevices and hissing beach grass. Not another soul. Yet I was called. The dunes called. Knees irradiated where I knelt, I busied myself without a thought, clawing out a shallow trench the depth of my body, then lay back into it, managed to cover myself toes to chin, staring up at the chalky light of mid-day. A whooshing in my ears like the sea. If someone had been there, had seen, there would have been only a little bird-girl's face in the dunes, unremarkable as an abandoned pie. A face in the dunes at the end of the world. No one came to see.

October 31

This shouldn't matter. It shouldn't matter at all to me that this is Halloween. The children of Wells Village have every right to be up and ghoulishly about. But of course I cannot this time be manning the front door, pressing quarter-size Milky Ways into little expectant palms. Single glimpse of my spectral, tufty head and a child would be off Halloween for life.

Instead, depressingly, J. has dragooned two tight-lipped fifth formers to tend our trick-or-treaters while he is conferring in his office about mess after mess.

Was Halloween ever a joy? I remember Brian when he was very little, three or four, alternately mystified and terrified to be out on the street, his hand tight in mine as we passed dark clusters of child zombies under the street lights. One year a freakish mask of green rubber sent him around the bend. One time, I remember, he was a mouse. I drew whiskers on his cheeks with eyeliner and darkened the tip of his nose, but I'm not sure he knew he was a mouse. For a few years running he was a "bum," which meant lashing himself into some huge shirt or jacket of John's or mine and blacking his cheeks. I remember scanning his countenance for a hint of pleasure when he arrived home. At twelve or thirteen he was done with Halloween and, I think, relieved. Poor children. To have to endure Halloween, scouts, school.

Downstairs in the hall, two uncomfortable boys are distributing bite-sized chocolate bars to children they will never know.

November 1

Still the awful pressure up into my chest.

But the day is bright blue beyond the mullions, and a hard wintry sun sets a few remaining leaves on fire. I would like to kick and swish through dry leaves on the walk. I would like to breathe that cold air deep, deep into my bunched lungs. It's morning but the light looks like afternoon. This weather is all about what's coming, seems to be hurrying up the holiday darkness.

I've been thinking about flight, about snuggling into a compartment of a train, roaring and chugging southward through mountain tunnels, through Switzerland, through Italy, from snow field to greenscape, from rock to warm earth, sun glinting on water, swans in silhouette against the dazzling facets.

November 2

Tried reading Powell this a.m., *Books Do Furnish a Room*. Deadly grim, of course, good as ever, but the more vividly I saw old Books Bagshaw or Mr. Deacon or Widmerpool making their way down familiar streets, the achingly sadder I felt. Powell knows how to call up the irretrievable past. That's it. For me there is only irretrievable past. Such crying. I did not believe I could stop. A medicinal effect? New mental territory?

Connie asks if I'm all right. I say I'm not very comfortable, which is more or less true but not at all related to my convulsive sobbing. It's important to Connie that crying have a clear, assignable cause. She restacks my pillows, gives me a sedative, a little cup of ice chips. There, there, Meg. All better? You're just suffering a little bout of impending death.

I want J. to come home. I want him to talk and talk and talk to me, and I don't need to say a single thing back. B., I feel I've lived a long time today.

November 3

New pitch of wrongness—same pitch, all one note.

Thought I was through this a.m. in the awful dawn light. Whoever defined life as pulse, as breath? It's neither. It's so much more elemental. It's a hum, a vibration of particles smaller than particles, and when you're finished and all wrong, the hum is grating and somehow off, and because it is off, it chafes and burns in waves, everywhere and nowhere, every tingling cell of the skin alive with it, skull, throat, pelvis, the arches of my feet. The thing alive in me now is cancer. I can only register. Sour, sulfurous and so wrong.

November 5

Sweet letter from nephew Hugh, wishing me well, of course knowing better.

Every message is now titanic, letters even more so than bedside visits because letters are disembodied. I see Hugh as physically enormous, energetic and mobile beyond my imagining. What does he picture when he pictures cancerous Aunt Meg in her schoolhouse sick bed? Glinting glasses and a bird beak, framed by pillow case. No, that's me picturing. Hugh wouldn't picture me at all, not if he's as whole and well as I think he is. He would avert mind's eye, hug the bright and hopeful shore.

Damn you, Hugh, and your pitch-perfect courtesy and your safe distance. I can hear Val's cooing pleas to weigh in with poor old Auntie Meg.

Not your fault, lovely admirable boy. It's not for you to know that for months I have cast my nets and cast my nets for Brian, for the shambling length of him, for even some word of him, and he is, I know, beyond lost, gone from me. Hugh's sweet gesture mocks my loss.

Brian is away, presumably moving about somewhere, distancing himself still further. But that is not how it feels. He feels a still and looming presence. He grows and glows before me. I see him in dazzling white places, on white sand, in white cities, in white clothes, under skies scorched white by the sun. There, wispy as gauze, but there, and it is I who shrink away from him. That's what this dying is—it is dying away from Brian.

Give me a day of you. Give me an hour of you. I would without a complaint take any kind of hour. Let me have you home again, dropped in for a night's sleep and change of clothes at Little House. I'll take you slouched over the breakfast table, hair matted and drooped low over your brow. Let me take in with a painter's greed your denim shirt over pale denim shirt, your jeans broken at your bent knee like some kind of hinge. You could not keep from me my pleasure in your lovely skin, John's boy-face in your bones. You cannot hide your eyes, grey, then blue, pooling with something, quick to disengage. Let me have your voice, that new voice, surprising and deep, never mind the words. I need no words. When you were thirteen and I could count the ribs on your back and chest, when your legs were stilts, all knee-knob and feet, the walnut of your Adam's apple moved with your talk, and your voice was wondrously like, I used to tease you, waxed paper over a comb. I am vibrating with that voice now. My heart, no, something more cavernous than my heart, is opening to that voice and, more, to the deeper, cello tone it learned to make when you drawled 'so-o-o,' or 'I don't know.' I hear it. I feel the tone of it on my skin, *o* sounds, saying 'not now,' or 'no.' Be here, sprawl here on this bed. Let me see you, lying back in the cockpit of Valmar, long brown fingers loose over the jib sheet, the blades of your shin, your knees knocked apart. I could look at you, all distraction, the wind in your hair, until the world goes dark.

Once I could tell you, gather your little bird body into me and tell you that you were my good, sweet baby. I never stopped needing that. Did I ever tell you, tell J., tell anyone how much I hated losing you to your school clothes, to the gloomy, gangling doubt of being a Young Man, a Wells boy, my lovely stick-bird muffled and armored by his crested blazer and regimental tie. And— crazy boy, crazy world—you knew it. You knew I ached for you beyond all words, and since there was no practical way for it to be otherwise, for you still to be my good sweet baby, you let me know you were forever lost to me. You made those necessary little distances vast. You willed that, maddening boy. You confined yourself in other rooms, rooms where I knew you were. You left the table early, began begging off all former pleasures. You asked your father if you could live in the dorm and let dorm master after dorm master write to us about your puzzling isolation there. I am sure you knew. I felt you knew I needed the throbbing bass of unknowable music behind your closed door, sniffs and signs of you, the steam of your shower on a mirror, the chalky trail of toothpaste spit into the blue porcelain, something deeper than the scent of you in your damp towels, your socks and tee shirts in the hamper. A phrase, the least phrase from you at the piano and I, from whatever perch in the house, would freeze fast, hold my breath. That was the very promise of heaven for me: you fingering music into the air, the very idea of you making Brian-marked things in the world. Oh, you knew I needed that. Too much, was it? If you gave that up to me, would you disappear? Is offering up to mother the death of a son? Why, please? Why such cruelty. Is holding back the death of the mother? What did I do but love you? I felt you swell and fill me and then gave you up. Up and out. I was just *friendly*, Brian, I was just nice. You could have been any old way in the world, any old way with me. I would have been thrilled if you had shocked me. I would have worn exasperation like a badge of honor. You stayed quiet. You learned to keep to other rooms, to rise from the piano and walk away without a sound.

I no longer go into your still room hoping to rest my eyes or finger tips on an object you held dear. There are only things you left—the old globe, someone's lacrosse stick, records I'm not sure you liked. In the closet, school blazer, a herringbone jacket, grey flannels, khakis. Not a trace of you.

So why are you here, somehow moving in and out of me with every sick breath? Without moving a finger tip, I am still forever gathering you into me, my good sweet baby, gathering you in, lowering my cheek to meet the warm rose talc of your baby skull, my fingers moving over the silky milky flesh of your arm, the little cushions of your wrists. Brian, your sweet skull cradled into my neck. I had that, I had that, I had you. Be forever there, gathered into me, my good sweet baby.

November 7

Conference here. A change in the morphia. I keep coming and going. Ice chips no good. Drying up.

November 8

New morphia takes me away, but then I come back. Not much breath for Gwen or even J. Told Gwen today where to put book-y when I'm done. Made her walk into the good guest room and promise me she knew the place on the shelf. Very careful about this. She must think I'm mad.

November 10

J. here all afternoon. Darkness falls over us. I fade away and wake to him, each time darker. J. so grey and spent, all bones himself. See what I've done.

November 12

Letters to Brian, J. finished. I watch Connie put them in my jewel box. As if she is slipping me into the dark box to wait.

November 15

This must be the end of you, b. Too sad to bear, but better, don't you think, a period than feeble elipses.

Clever for the last time. Let the record show that when the body dried up and failed, there was at the end a little rasp of sere cleverness. Which is all cleverness is.

Cleverness, the words themselves are precisely nothing. They are meta-life, instead of life. In the beginning was not the word. The word was always instead. No doubt at all. Consider my credentials.

A baby's new skin, new skull, that is life. A cheek on a cheek. A fingertip tracing the spine's nubs, loving that, loving period.

I wonder—had words failed me, would there only have been fingertips and what, with grace, they found? Love at my fingertips, if only words had failed me.

Fail me now, please. At any rate I am saying good-bye to you. Giving up, failing words. Something tenacious in me doesn't quite want to send you away to the guest-room shelf with four or five perfectly clean white pages going vacant. Do dying thieves itch to pull one more little job?

I release you, waiting pages. Be for some browser white hymns, sighs.

There was John, Brian. Sun on water.

This I know.